Sign up for our newsletter to hear
about new and upcoming releases.

www.ylva-publishing.com

Always a Love Song

CHARLEY CLARKE

Chapter One

Then

WHEN ALEX LOOKED BACK ON this night in two or five or ten years, she'd remember it as perfect. What else could it be when they were eighteen—or near enough, in her case—freshly graduated, and on top of the world? Not literally, of course. They weren't even on top of the building. They sat on the stage in the empty Wentworth Theater, a six-pack and a battery-operated camping lantern between them. The theater had been closed for a year, but Bridget had snuck out of her house enough times to have learned a thing or two.

Their pocket of light made the rest of the black theater even eerier, but nothing could touch Alex when she was with Bridget. Her best friend. Someone who could be more than a friend. One day. But Alex wasn't going to push it. She was just going to keep on loving Bridget because loving made her feel like a sun spreading warmth to everyone she met. Didn't even matter if Bridget loved her back.

"You're going to be a big star one day," Alex said. "You're going to be up here on this stage, and I'm going to be in the front row clapping the loudest."

Bridget bumped her shoulder. "I wouldn't have it any other way."

With her golden hair, sparkling smile, and glowing personality, maybe it was Bridget who was the sun.

"But we're going to have adventures first," Bridget said. "Lots of them, starting with college."

Alex's smile fell away, and she bit her lip. It wasn't that she wasn't excited for the year to come. It was just that they were going to change. That was what growing up was all about.

"What is it?" Bridget asked in a whisper. "You can tell me."

"It's just..." Alex sighed. "What if we grow apart?"

"We won't," Bridget said, fidgeting with the corner of the beer carton, an idle smile on her lips as she regarded Alex. "I'm not worried."

"You're not? Not even a little bit?"

"Nope."

Alex found her chest lightening. Because change could be good for a relationship. Change meant growth.

Besides, they were Alex and Bridget. Inseparable.

Bridget pulled one leg up under herself. "I can't imagine my life without you, and now, I don't have to."

And all of a sudden, Alex couldn't help it. She couldn't fight the fuzziness that welled up in her chest and threatened to explode. She surged forward and kissed Bridget's cheek.

Even in the dim lantern light, Bridget's answering blush was apparent. "Why'd you do that?"

"Because..." Because it felt right. Because they were best friends. Because words sometimes weren't enough. "You're my favorite person. Ever."

"Yeah?"

"Yeah."

Bridget grinned. "Well, you're mine, too. But for a scholarship athlete, your aim's pitiful."

"My aim?"

Bridget closed the gap between them again, but this time, lips met lips. It wasn't Alex's first kiss, but it was the first one that meant something. This wasn't fumbling around behind the bleachers or in the corner of a house party. It wasn't even open-mouthed. It was just soft, warm pressure and the feeling of Bridget's smile beneath her own.

Yeah. Definitely a perfect night.

Now

"Music's golden girl Bridget Callahan has broken her silence about her fiancé's shocking infidelity," the entertainment anchor on TV said.

Alex finished the chai she was making and handed it off to her customer, then picked up the remote and switched the channel to a women's golf match, but not before catching a glimpse of the screen, which showed a smiling Bridget in a stunning green dress on the red carpet. The Grammys. This past year. Not that Alex kept track of that stuff.

She had a café, a bar, and a brewery to run. Her life didn't have room for celebrity gossip.

"Hey, Alex," Lu said, loudly enough to draw the attention of everyone in the café. Even Benny, Alex's pit bull, looked up from where he was lounging beneath Lu's feet. Jordan and Owen filled out the rest of their unofficially reserved corner table, with their daughter, Keiko, in a stroller that Owen rocked with one foot.

"Refill?" Alex asked.

Lu, dressed in her park ranger uniform, shook her head and gestured to the television. "Who do you think's going to win this tournament?"

"Oh, definitely Culey," Owen said. "She's been on fire all year."

Alex filled a to-go cup with hot water. Even though the reminder of Bridget's success no longer hurt, her friends couldn't seem to get out of the routine. "I wouldn't be so sure," she said. "I'd put my money on Park."

"Boo," Jordan said, waving a dismissive hand. "She's what, thirty-nine? She can't keep up with these eighteen- and nineteen-year-olds. She's three strokes behind Culey right now."

"She's a master. She'll pull through." Alex shrugged. "Besides, the old ones are the sure things. They're solid. They won't choke under pressure."

"And let us not forget," Lu said, "that though she may be a veteran in athletic terms, she's by no means actually old."

Alex dropped a fresh Earl Grey teabag into the cup and took it over to the table. She planted a kiss on her goddaughter's forehead before handing the drink to Lu. "For your shift."

Lu accepted it with a grimace. "If I had known this job would involve weekends, I never would have accepted."

"Yes, you would have," Owen said matter-of-factly. "Because, despite the weekends, you love it and you wouldn't be happy without it."

Lu threw a sugar packet at him. "This is why I need new friends. You guys know me too well."

"Yeah, fifteen years will do that," Jordan said, leaning back with a sage expression.

"You can advertise for new friends after your shift," Alex said, waving her towel at Lu. "Don't be late!"

"Fine. Fine." Lu grumbled as she adjusted her ball cap. "Put it on my tab, will ya, sweetheart?"

Alex swatted her with the towel. "Get out of here."

"Stop trying to hurry me." Lu looked at her watch. "I have at least six more minutes."

Jordan pushed an empty chair out from the table with her foot. "Sit a spell, friend. Make the most of Lu's six minutes."

"I've got customers," Alex said suspiciously. Her friends were a common fixture in both the café and the bar next door, but they usually didn't interfere with her job. What were they up to?

"You've also got very competent employees," Owen said. "Now sit."

With an exaggerated sigh, she complied. "What?"

Jordan lifted an accusing eyebrow. "You reached for that remote awfully fast, there."

Alex rolled her eyes. "I hate gossip. Just because she's a celebrity doesn't mean she doesn't deserve a private life."

"Okay, but did you listen any before you changed the channel?"

"Why would I?" She had, sort of, but she'd been too distracted to really process any of it.

Owen swiveled his laptop toward her. On the screen was an article with the headline "America's Sweethearts' Shocking Break-Up," accompanied by individual pictures of Bridget and Patrick Norwood, Hollywood's current hottest commodity, and a third photograph of the two together at his latest movie premiere.

Alex shoved down the eruption of anger. She was past that. Bridget's romantic entanglements didn't affect her. Sure, she knew he'd proposed to her on stage three months ago, but only because everyone did. It was impossible to escape Bridget Callahan fever.

Talk about irritating.

She gave a disinterested shrug. "So?"

"*So* they broke up, like, the day after they got engaged, and *she* wanted to keep it a secret," Owen said, leaning forward eagerly.

"What's your point?"

"Our point," Jordan said, "is that maybe she doesn't have as perfect a life as she wants everyone to believe."

"Perfect comeuppance for a perfect bitch," Lu said, blowing on her tea.

Owen leaned over the stroller to cover Keiko's ears even though she'd fallen fast asleep.

"Language, Lu," Alex said as she got to her feet and straightened her apron.

Lu raised an eyebrow. "What? Bitch?"

"No," Alex said with a smirk. "Where'd you learn the word 'comeuppance'?"

Even surrounded by people, Bridget was alone. Or, at least, it felt that way. This was what her life had become, just a still body in a sea of constantly moving people. Television studio workers scurried around prepping for the show. Her agent, Pippa, chattered on the phone, making decisions on her behalf. And Max, her best friend and songwriting partner, was too caught up in flirting with his makeup artist to even glance her way.

"I want to go home," Bridget said. The decision came out of nowhere. Or everywhere, maybe, informed by five long years of loneliness and heartache, and exacerbated by this mess of a breakup. It wasn't loud enough for anyone but Pippa or Kit, her makeup artist, to hear.

Kit gave her a sympathetic pout, but her hand never wavered as she applied lipstick.

Without taking her eyes from her smartphone, Pippa said, "It's a measly interview. You've done a million, and every one is GIF-ably adorable."

Bridget waited until Kit moved to eyeshadow to say, "It's the first one I've done since..." Since the whole world found out she'd destroyed the perfect relationship with the perfect guy. Perfect was in the eye of the beholder, though, wasn't it? Not so perfect if she spent the entire time thinking about someone else.

Pippa finally looked at her. "I know," she said, her tone unusually gentle. "But it's a breakup, not the end of the world. It happens all the time between celebrities. The truth had to come out eventually, and you'll get through it with grace, like you always do."

Bridget did a short breathing exercise. It didn't calm her as much as usual, but it helped. "After this, though, I'm serious about going home."

"You're supposed to be writing new songs," Pippa said, slipping into her stern voice again.

Max, done with his makeup, hopped out of his chair to join them. "What do you think we're playing today?"

Pippa crossed her arms. "One song does not an album make."

"I have been writing. *We* have," Bridget said. "And I'll keep writing when I go home. I just … I really need a break, Pip."

Max gave Pippa his calculated puppy-dog eyes. She was one of the few people—besides Bridget, of course—proven immune to them, but he tried anyway. "She's the hardest working musician in the industry. She deserves a break, wouldn't you agree?"

Pippa sighed. "And you'll be accompanying her to work on next year's top album?"

"We can write over Skype and stuff," Bridget suggested, not wanting to pressure him into spending time in the middle of nowhere, even if she desperately wanted him there.

All ease and nonchalance, Max grinned the dimpled grin that drove their fans wild. "I've always wanted to visit Pennsylvania."

"You know I'm nowhere near the Liberty Bell, right?" Bridget asked. Outside of Pennsylvania, that was the only thing the state was known for. And Punxsutawney Phil. Everyone loved him. Inside the state, it was pierogi and sports and remnants of steel. Fun and rich in history, but not exactly a thrill a minute.

Max groaned.

She smacked his arm. "If you're good, I'll take you to a Steelers game."

"I thought you didn't like football."

She'd loved it once—in her old life. Sunday afternoons of full living rooms and jerseys in church and eating until you were stuffed. "Everyone there loves football. It's a rule."

"Then it's settled. I'll book the tickets," Pippa said before waltzing off.

A stagehand replaced her. "Five minutes, you two."

Kit ran a lint brush over each of their shoulders, then stepped back to assess them. "All done! Break a leg!"

"Thanks," Bridget said. Once Kit walked away, she snaked an arm around Max's waist and leaned her head on his shoulder. "And thank *you*."

"What are best friends for?"

"Um…" She put a finger to her chin and pretended to think. "Writing kick-ass songs that win awards and making me delicious baked goods and saving me from making terrible life decisions." She snorted. If only he'd talked some sense into her five years ago. Then again, they had only been acquaintances back then.

"Co-writing," he amended. "Now let's get out there and show the world what real songwriting looks like."

She straightened. "Right."

All told, the situation could have been much worse. This appearance on *The Mikayla Miles Show* had been scheduled before the news broke the day before. Bridget was lucky that Mikayla, one of America's favorite daytime hosts, tended to sympathize with her guests. It was a good place to break big news. Or explain it.

Like why she'd broken up with the nation's most famous and beloved actor after he'd proposed to her on her first world tour.

They made it three minutes without a mention.

Then: "I have to ask, Bridget," Mikayla said, looking sincere. "You know I have to ask. You've been pretty quiet lately, working on your new album, but a lot has been going on. You and Patrick Norwood got engaged on your tour stop in Paris on stage in front of a screaming crowd. But yesterday, you released a statement saying you're no longer together. So, what happened to America's sweethearts?"

"You know, after we got engaged," Bridget said, "we had a long conversation, and we realized our visions of the future didn't match up. That's all."

"So, there was no cheating involved?"

"None whatsoever. I asked him for some time, and he gave it to me, but I didn't want to keep him from moving on."

"And the pictures?"

"Were taken last week, after we'd been broken up for months."

Mikayla looked at the audience. "You heard it straight from Bridget Callahan herself, people. There is no need to demonize Patrick Norwood."

She turned back to Bridget. "Now for a harder question, Bridget. Do you still love him?"

Bridget sighed quietly. How terrible it was to break another person's heart in order to heal your own. She only wished the pain had more to do with him than with her first love. She smiled. Five years had taught her how to do it convincingly even if her heart wasn't in it. "Of course I do. Just because something doesn't work out doesn't mean your feelings dissolve in an instant."

"Thank you for your honesty," Mikayla said. "I know this must be difficult to talk about."

"Unfortunately, I'm a bit desensitized to people overanalyzing my personal life."

"I'm sure. Who knows? Maybe you can turn it into a song down the road."

Bridget laughed lightly. "Maybe."

"And speaking of songs," Mikayla said, "Bridget's songwriting partner, the very adorable Max Ocampo is here, and they're going to play for us. Are you ready, Bridget?"

Bridget smacked her hands down on her armrests. "I'm ready."

"Well, don't be too ready. We've got a commercial break now." Mikayla addressed the camera. "Stay tuned for the premiere of a brand-new song from the one and only Bridget Callahan!"

Bridget released her breath, and a bucketload of tension, when the red light winked out.

Mikayla leaned forward to touch her arm. "Hey, was that all right? I hate asking such personal questions."

"Yeah, it's good. I'm good," Bridget said. "I know you have to do it."

"Try not to be so famous, would you?"

"Well, the plan is to lie low a while, so we'll see."

"Good luck with that." Mikayla tilted her head toward the stage. "You should probably get over there."

"Sure, sure." She stood, wiped her palms off on her jeans, and joined Max on stage, where he perched on a stool, holding an acoustic guitar.

"Look at you, coming through unscathed."

Bridget sat at the piano bench. "Always do."

"Are you sure you want to sing this one? Not too late to change."

Bridget ran through an arpeggio. It couldn't be too late—for closure, at least, if not for a second chance. Her songs had always been personal. This one was no different, really. "No. We're doing this one."

"Okay."

"Thirty seconds," someone called.

Mikayla gave them a thumbs-up from the other side of the set. Max returned it. Bridget merely nodded. She took five deep breaths before the camera light blinked back on. Mikayla introduced them once more, and finally, Max began plucking out the intro.

Bridget lost herself in the music.

After the show, Bridget pulled out her phone and texted someone she hadn't spoken to in years, hoping her number was still the same.

I'm about to tell all my followers I'm going back home for a much-needed break. I didn't want you to find out from anyone else.

Then, as an afterthought: *And this is Bridget. In case you lost my number.*

The reply came a few minutes later: *I know who it is. Thanks for telling me.*

You're okay with it? Bridget asked.

This response was quicker. *It's your hometown, too. I'm sorry if you stayed away all this time because of me.*

Bridget let go of the breath she was holding. *You always were a better person than me. Maybe I'll see you around?*

This time, there was no reply.

Chapter Two

Then

BRIDGET FLOPPED ONTO ALEX'S TINY twin bed as Alex peeled off her sweatshirt and hung it in her closet. Most of their friends, including Alex's roommate, had gone home for fall break, but they'd elected to stay on campus to spend some time together that didn't include homework or a dozen other people.

"I'm stuffed," Bridget said, hands on her stomach, eyes closed.

"We could've brought home leftovers, you know," Alex said.

"But it looked and tasted so good. No regrets."

Alex's soft laugh put a smile on Bridget's face, too. Even in the tiny freshman dorm room, she sounded too far away. Bridget popped an eye open to see Alex perched on the other bed. Hmm.

Scooting up so she was sitting against the headboard, Bridget patted the spot next to her. It was a squeeze, but they'd spent a lot of time in twin beds together. "Come 'ere."

Alex curled her hands around the edge of the mattress, staring at the floor without answering.

Bridget considered her girlfriend—her beautiful, intelligent, confident girlfriend. Adjusting to college life had been difficult and sometimes weird. Bridget missed home a lot more than she'd thought she would, especially considering they were only an hour away, but Alex's presence lessened the sting. Because Alex *was* home, in a way. Alex made Bridget feel comfortable and cared for.

So, why, all of a sudden, was she acting so distant?

"I thought we stayed here to spend extra time together without distractions," Bridget said quietly. "Do you want me to go back to my room?"

"What? No. No, I don't want you to go." Alex injected bravado into her voice, but she still couldn't quite meet Bridget's eye.

Maybe she was just tired. Or itching to get a jump on all the homework she'd have to do on Sunday. If that was it, though, it wouldn't be the first time they'd spent the night quietly working on different projects.

No, this was something more. This was something new, which meant something had to have changed, and the only thing that had changed was…

Oh.

"This is the first time we'll be alone without roommates. Maybe you think I have…expectations?"

Alex didn't say anything, only took a deep breath.

So that was it. Bridget, who'd always been more comfortable with her body and with physicality, didn't mind waiting. Not for Alex. While five months may be a long time to other eighteen-year-olds, Bridget wasn't going to jeopardize something this special.

She moved to the edge of the bed, where she could face Alex. "I know we haven't really talked about it, so if I'm off base, let me know. But…I don't think I am."

Alex shook her head.

"So, let's talk about it." Bridget turned her hand palm-up and rested it on her knee within Alex's reach. She wouldn't push in any way, but she craved contact. "I'm sorry I made you feel like that."

"You didn't," Alex said quickly.

"Then what did?"

"Only every single book and movie ever made," Alex replied, chuckling weakly. But she reached out her hand to hold Bridget's.

Despite the unexpected heaviness of the moment, Bridget smiled. She loved holding Alex's hand—even when it was slightly clammy.

"I didn't want you to get bored," Alex said, her voice barely above a whisper. "I didn't want to be that girlfriend who made you wait so long that you left."

Bridget couldn't help but be upset by that. She should've done more to reassure Alex. "Can I sit by you?"

Alex nodded.

Bridget moved to the other bed, keeping one hand in Alex's and sliding the other to her back. "I'm never going to pressure you into having sex before you're ready, and if I do, I deserve to be kicked to the curb. Got it?"

Alex squeezed her hand.

"Good. I just like spending time with you, baby, no matter what we do. I've watched you do homework and loved it."

That earned her a tiny laugh.

"All I want to do tonight is cuddle and watch a movie. We aren't going to do anything more than that until you want to. Hell, if you never want to, we can figure that out, too."

"No, I want to, I think," Alex said shyly. "Just not tonight."

"Definitely not tonight." Bridget pressed a kiss into Alex's hair. "I've got two promises for you. Are you ready?"

"Mm-hmm."

"We'll never do anything unless we're both comfortable with it."

Alex leaned her head on Bridget's shoulder. "Okay."

"And when the time comes," Bridget said, "I'll take care of you. I'll always take care of you, Lex."

Now

"Mom!" Bridget exclaimed as she and Max exited the rental SUV.

Evelyn Callahan met her in the driveway with a bear hug. "It's been far too long since you've been home."

Bridget rolled her eyes, grateful her mom couldn't see. "And here, I thought we'd make it inside before you chastised me."

"Oh, hush," Evelyn said. "I love you, but you deserve it for staying away so long."

"I've flown you out to visit me multiple times each year!"

Evelyn ignored her in favor of hugging Max. "Max! How are you, dear?"

He grinned. "Doing well. Thank you, Mrs. C."

"Come in. Come in." Evelyn waved them toward the house. "I'm sure you two are hungry from traveling all day."

Bridget and Max grabbed their suitcases from the trunk before following, but Bridget only made it to the foyer before she stopped. Little touches were different—a painting here, a lamp there—but the majority of the house was unchanged. A wooden staircase covered in a Persian runner led up to the second floor. The dining room off to the left featured a rectangular table that seated twelve. It was a bit less crowded than it used to be, what with Bridget's dad gone and Bridget herself a coward who never came home. Her brothers were still in the area, though, one thirty minutes away and the other an hour, so the table still got good use.

She regretted not coming home sooner. But it had never been about her family. Even now, though, she was afraid to examine her true motives, afraid to find Alex there, at the heart of it all.

"The house looks great, Mom," she said.

"And it smells like cookies," Max said.

"Fresh from the oven," Evelyn said with a smile, "but you'll have to wait for them to cool."

Bridget wandered into the living room while Max and her mom chatted. The TV was a lot bigger, but the couch was still the same brown one she loved so much. Beneath it, nestled beside the stereo, were two CDs. Her own. She pulled them out. Attached to the front of each was a sticky note in her own hand, both addressed to Alex. Hot tears welled in her eyes.

She strode back into the foyer and held up the CDs. "You never gave them to her?" She hated how small her voice sounded.

Evelyn wrapped an arm around Bridget's shoulders. "I tried, honey."

So she didn't want them. Of course she didn't. Bridget wouldn't take anything from a selfish ex, either.

"This is probably a good time to tell you that in the basement, there are a few boxes of your stuff from the apartment," Evelyn said. "She couldn't take everything, and I didn't quite know what to do with it."

Bridget choked out a half-sob, half-laugh. More shit that she'd run away from all those years ago. This whole trip was going to be an exercise in delayed pain. "Why would now be a good time to tell me that?"

"You have to rip off the Band-Aid all at once, Bridgie."

Bridget bit her bottom lip. "I'd rather just find a stronger Band-Aid."

Evelyn chuckled. "You can't keep running away from the things that hurt you. You've got to face her sometime."

Bridget knew that. She also knew that as soon as she saw Alex again, she'd want to run straight back into her arms. The problem was that Alex wanted nothing to do with her, and Bridget couldn't blame her.

"Well, why don't I show you to the guest room?" Evelyn said to Max.

His room was the first at the top of the stairs. It used to be Marcus and Ian's room before they'd moved out for good. Now, the sports and movie posters had been replaced by plain yellow walls, and the twin beds had been swapped for a single queen-sized one with a dark blue comforter. It was comfortable without being too inviting or interesting.

Max set down his suitcase at the foot of the bed. "Looks great, Mrs. C. Thanks."

"Oh, Max, you're so easy to please," Evelyn said, looking pleased, too.

Bridget dragged her bags to her old bedroom. She stopped in the doorway. It was so...unremarkable. And so much the same, even though the walls boasted a new coat of light gold paint and her mom had swapped out most of the furniture. A queen bed covered by a striped red duvet. A bookshelf. A desk bare of a laptop or papers. An old guitar in a stand in the corner.

This tiny room was imbued with so many memories, mostly good. Middle-school sleepovers. Playing songs for Alex on her very first guitar. Late mornings after high-school parties. The first time they'd had sex. All the other times they'd had sex in this bed. The times they'd cuddled and watched movies instead.

Some memories not so good. The week after her father died. The crushing emptiness of the room when they'd fought and Bridget wanted to call the only person who didn't want to hear from her.

Even with all the trappings changed and Bridget's belongings gone, Alex was in every single atom of this room. Fuck, she couldn't do this. She'd just sleep on the couch.

With a grunt, she hefted her duffel and her suitcase and headed back downstairs.

Evelyn's voice followed her. "Honey, where are you going?"

"Downstairs." Bridget set her suitcase at the foot of the couch. This could do. Maybe a couch wasn't the best choice for an extended stay, but she had the TV, and the kitchen was right there.

"With your bags?" Evelyn asked.

14

"Yeah," Bridget called.

"Oh." Rapid footsteps down the stairs. Then her mom was in the living room, hands on her hips. "You won't get very much rest here, you know."

"Well, I can't..." Bridget swallowed down the tightness in her throat. "I can't stay there."

Evelyn hummed. "I thought I'd changed it enough that it wouldn't matter. You'll switch with Max, then."

A surge of gratitude welled in Bridget. Her refusal to come home had to have been tough on her mom, and yet Evelyn hadn't pushed, and she wouldn't push. She wouldn't because she already knew. She knew Bridget's heart was a shattered mess clumsily taped together, and she knew it was all Bridget's own fault. Her greatest mistake and her greatest regret.

She should keep a count of how many times she got a breath away from letting the tears fall this trip.

"Yeah, Mom," she managed. "I think that's a good idea."

At the opposite end of the bar, Riley jerked her chin in the direction of the door. "Incoming."

Lu, Jordan, and Owen walked in, Owen pushing a sleeping Keiko in her stroller. Benny barked and padded over to greet them, tail wagging.

"Hey," Alex called from behind the bar. "The usual starter?"

"Yes, please!" Jordan said.

The group sat at their usual table in the back. Alex poured Life on the Berm draft into three steins and brought them over, leaving Riley and Hunter to man the bar. Benny had already settled beneath the table by Lu's feet.

"Thanks, Al," Lu said, sipping the foam from the top of hers.

"So, we heard She Who Must Not Be Named is officially back in town," Owen said.

Jordan elbowed him in the side, but Alex just smiled. "Have you guys seen her? Fawned all over her yet?"

The three exchanged glances, guilty enough that she threw up her hands. "What? Just say it."

"Is that allowed?" Jordan asked meekly. "Fawning?"

Alex rolled her eyes. "Aren't you a little old for that?"

"You're never too old for a good bop," Owen said, "and she's got a few."

"Yeah, and she's also got enough people fawning over her."

"Actually," Jordan said, "from what I can tell, people are trying to be respectful of her space. She's on vacation, after all."

"Still, if you three make a big deal about it, she'll get an even bigger head."

"Then she won't even be able to fit through the door," Owen said.

Alex snorted. Like that was a concern. "I doubt she'll be coming in here."

Lu laughed, earning a glare from Jordan. "What? Saying you won't run into your ex is, like, the first rule of dealing with exes. It dooms you."

"Thank you for that brilliant advice, Lu," Alex said, a little too harshly.

"Don't be sore. I'm just looking out for you."

"You don't have to anymore. I'm a big girl." When she caught sight of their skeptical faces, Alex took a deep breath. "Look, guys, relax. I'm fine."

Before any of them could respond, Riley said from the bar, "I'm going on my break, Al."

Alex nodded. "Sure."

"Hey, Benny. Want to go for a walk?"

The pit bull lifted his head at the last word. When Riley walked toward the door, he ran after her.

"Thanks, Ri," Alex called.

"Don't mention it. See you in half an hour."

Lu leaned forward. "The whole town's talking, you know."

"Oh, yeah?" Alex said nonchalantly. "What about?"

"As far as we can tell," Owen said, "half of them are thrilled the prodigal daughter has returned."

"And the other half?"

"Out for the prodigal daughter's blood," Jordan said, the corners of her mouth twitching with the beginnings of a grin. "For...you know."

"Yeah," Alex said. For breaking her heart. The whole town had watched their romance blossom and later implode. "Well, I'll be sure to send half the town thank-you cards when she leaves."

Lu took a long drink. "So, what'll it be? Should we tar and feather her?"

God, she didn't need them to come *this* far over to her side. Bridget was still someone Alex had once loved. She rested her forearms on the table. "How would you guys treat her if I weren't in the equation?"

Jordan sighed. "We'd flip out. In a good way."

"Seeing her after five years?" Lu added. "Yeah, she was our friend, too."

"Okay, well," Alex said with a shrug, "maybe you should do that, then."

Max strummed an A chord. "What are you thinking for this line?"

"Which one?" Bridget asked, consulting the lyrics she'd scrawled into a notebook on the plane.

They sat on adjacent stools in the basement studio Bridget's parents had built when she was fifteen, and they realized she was more than a little serious about music. The glass box wasn't big enough to fit a whole band, just a keyboard, a couple guitars, and a drum kit if they wanted to be ambitious. It was perfect for just her and Max, which was how they had started. Sometimes, she thought that was how they would end, too. The two of them and their guitars. What a quartet they made.

"'Her name was Sorrow,'" Max said. He strummed the chord again and tried out a vocal line.

Bridget shook her head. "No, not quite like that." She tried an A minor and sang a variation. "'Her name was Sorrow. She had my face.'"

"You want harmony on that?"

"I don't know yet. Maybe on the next two lines?"

"'Your name was Hope. You taught me grace'?"

"Yeah." She scribbled chord notations over the lyrics.

Max plucked out the melody. "Are we ever going to write a happy song again?"

"What are you talking about? We write happy songs all the time."

"'Up-tempo' and 'happy' aren't the same thing."

Bridget lifted her gaze to meet his. His brown eyes were full of concern. If she couldn't tell him about the turmoil she was feeling, she couldn't tell anyone.

"I'm trying," she said.

"I know, and I don't mean to push you."

"It's just a lot harder than I thought it'd be. Coming home."

He gave her a lopsided smile. "That's why I'm here."

"To help me mine past heartbreak to use for song lyrics?"

"Something like that, yeah." He tapped the body of his guitar. "I'm just saying. Maybe it's time to mine *my* heartbreak instead."

Bridget laughed. Maybe she *was* getting to be a broken record.

When Evelyn knocked on the studio window a moment later, they set down their guitars and came out to the main part of the basement. It wasn't much to look at—a wooden coffee table, a forest green futon, a flat-screen TV sitting on a chest against the opposite wall, and a pile of boxes in the corner.

"What's up, Mom?" Bridget asked.

Evelyn put her fists on her hips. "Is this how you're going to spend your entire vacation? Squirreling yourselves away in the basement?"

Bridget and Max exchanged a look, then, nodding, turned back to her mom.

"Pretty much," Bridget said. "It's our job, after all. Do you want my career to crash and burn because my next album flops?"

"No, but it's your first night here. You should show Max around town."

"You mean around the bowling alley, the liquor store, and the closed-down theater?" Bridget's voice caught on the last word. She cleared her throat to cover it up. Another place with inescapable memories.

Evelyn frowned. One day, and Bridget was driving her to that state of motherhood where worry for her adult children caused wrinkles. "All your friends are still here, Bridge," she said. "Owen and Jordan and Lu. You should get in touch with them on the Facebook."

"It's not *the* Facebook, Mom. It's just Facebook."

"Whatever it is, it doesn't mask the fact that you're twenty-eight years old and spending Friday night at your mother's house."

Max leaned a hip against the door frame of the studio. "I'm up for bowling or whatever. Is there a place to get a drink around here?"

Evelyn's expression lightened. "Now, there's a boy after my own spontaneous heart. You should be more like Max."

Bridget's jaw dropped while Max grinned.

"Anyway," Evelyn said, like she hadn't just mortally offended her only daughter, "there's a place called The Pothole. Good beer and good pizza, which is not something you can say for every small-town watering hole. It's on Main, right next to the café. You can't miss it."

Bridget shook off the evening chill as she followed Max into The Pothole, which, as her mom had warned her, was right next to the café. Just inside the door was a plaque proclaiming that the bar had been established in the memory of Calvin Marlowe, Alex's dad. She didn't even need to see the door leading to the café to extrapolate that Alex owned both.

She wiped shaky, sweaty palms on the thighs of her jeans. This was ridiculous. Absolutely ridiculous. She could get up on stage in front of sixty thousand people without batting an eye. She could perform on live television broadcasts across the country without an ounce of nerves.

She led Max to a booth against the wall, keeping her head down in case anyone she knew from before was here. If Alex hated her, surely they all did, too. She wasn't ready for that.

She fidgeted with the placemat as Max went to the bar to order two beers, and when he slid back into the booth with that tense expression, she just *knew*. Alex was here. Of course. Because she owned the place, which her mom had conveniently forgotten to mention.

"Isn't—" Max started to ask.

"Yes."

"And isn't—"

"Yes."

"Hmm." He paused. "Wow. Your mom's kind of a jerk."

"I can think of another word for it." Still, Bridget was a masochistic fuck, so after a long swig of admittedly delicious beer, she asked, "She's over there?"

Max nodded. "Yeah, she's over there."

Bridget risked a glance. Wrong move. Alex was in tight black jeans that showed off her amazing ass. Her black-and-blue plaid shirt was unbuttoned partway, revealing a black tank beneath, and the sleeves were rolled up to expose her forearms. Her very sinewy, fit forearms. Bridget groaned audibly. With regret, with want.

In a blink, her beer was all over the table. Bridget quickly righted the glass and grabbed a wad of napkins to sop up the mess.

"Shit, Bridge," Max said. "Let me grab something to help."

He disappeared and returned a minute later with a towel. After soaking up the spill, he gathered all the sopping napkins and took them to the bar.

Bridget let her head fall into her hands. Oh, God. Alex was here. She'd seen that. She *knew* Bridget was a mess.

"Hey," Max said when he returned. "No harm done."

"Lots of harm done, I think."

Max pushed a fresh glass toward her. "Were you always this nervous around her, or is it just because you haven't seen her in so long?"

"I haven't seen her since I broke her heart, Max. I'm allowed to be nervous. Besides, that shirt is just not fair. No one should be allowed to look that good in plaid."

He chuckled and sipped his drink. "This beer is really good. Maybe if you get yourself another one, it'll take your mind off how good she looks."

"I doubt it."

"So…is that why you came home? To win her back?"

Bridget locked her fingers together to keep herself from fidgeting. Did she? Was that the reason, buried beneath all the others, she refused to acknowledge? "I don't know."

"Well, maybe going to say hello would help you figure it out."

The blood drained from Bridget's face. "I can't."

"Bridget, you performed in front of the president."

"Oh, I miss him."

"You can face an ex-girlfriend."

"An ex-girlfriend who hates me."

Okay, so she'd go, and then what? If Alex asked how she was, what would she even say? *My bed is cold without you? My life is a mere semblance of a life without you?* How pathetic was that? She was her own person. She didn't need Alex to make her whole.

She *wanted* Alex, though.

There. Now she didn't have to spend the entirety of this trip lying to herself.

"You'll regret it if you don't," Max said, his focus already on the picture of his beer he was posting.

She forced a smile. He was right. He was always right. So, with a great big sigh, Bridget slid out of the booth and walked toward the bar.

After all this time, Alex felt it like an earthquake. Her world tilted on its axis when Bridget Callahan walked through the door of her bar, walked into her life for the first time in five years. Alex had had four days to brace herself, but four centuries wouldn't have been enough time to prepare. Her shoulders dropped as she dried out a glass with a rag.

Bridget looked good. Really good. Like, fuck, she didn't deserve to look that attractive. Her jeans were form-fitting, but not too tight, and her black sweater and red scarf were pleasantly fashionable without trying too hard. Plus, she had the golden glow of the famous, that carefree bearing that didn't let anything touch them. She walked in with Max Ocampo, whom Alex recognized from television and pictures, and they slid into a booth like they were meant to be here, like this small town was big enough to hold people as recognizable as they were.

Alex turned to a patron, got an order, and poured a drink, all while endeavoring to ignore the blonde in the corner. But Bridget's presence was magnetic, drawing Alex's attention repeatedly.

Ten minutes later, after Max cleaned up a spill at their table, Bridget finally looked up and caught Alex staring.

Don't come over. Don't come over. Don't come over.

She came over.

Alex turned away. She slid down to the other end of the bar, busying her hands with wiping down the counter.

A little ways down, Bridget leaned against the bar and cleared her throat.

"What can I do for you?" Hunter asked.

"Um, I don't know. What's your best drink?"

Relatively new, Hunter wasn't the best at recommendations, so of course he said the absolute wrong thing. "Well, we've got a pretty banging one called the Callahan."

"The Callahan?" Bridget asked, voice uncertain. Her gaze flickered to Alex.

Alex stiffened. *Build those walls up. Build them up high and strong.*

"Fun while it lasts, but you regret it in the morning," Alex said, a bite in the words. She and Lu had come up with the drink years ago. It'd been a lark. It'd been a coping mechanism. She'd never expected Bridget to come back, but now that she had, explaining it to her face sent a thrill through Alex.

"Right." Bridget let out a long breath, tapping her fingertips against the counter. "Okay, could I just get a beer, then?"

"What kind?"

"Whatever kind you give to people who just say 'a beer' and don't specify."

Hunter's forehead crinkled.

"Give her the usual, Hunt," Alex said, biting back a sigh. He could make this easier on all of them if he were a tad brighter.

"Oh. Right." He filled a stein with the house lager.

Alex turned away again.

"We should talk," Bridget said.

Alex's jaw jumped with tension. "I think we're five years past that point, actually," she said, and walked away before Bridget could respond.

Then the front door opened, and Benny trotted through, followed closely by Riley, her cheeks flushed from the evening chill. Benny raced over.

To Bridget.

"Benny!" Bridget held open her arms, and Benny jumped into them. She gave him a vigorous petting. "Oh, I've missed you, boy." As Benny licked her face, she laughed and said, "I know. I know. Hello to you, too."

"Traitor," Alex muttered.

Riley, who had joined her behind the bar, dug a teasing elbow into her side. "Someone's sore."

"She can have everything else," Alex said. "But she can't have Benny."

"Relax," Riley said. "She's not going to take him. He missed her. She missed him. But it's your bed he'll be sleeping in tonight."

"Mm." Alex still couldn't manage to smooth out the crease in her forehead. This was bad. This was very bad. Hardly thinking, she turned to Riley. "Will you pretend to be my girlfriend?"

Riley barked out a laugh.

"What?"

Riley lifted an eyebrow. "You promised you wouldn't turn into a hot mess when you saw her."

Alex crossed her arms. "I'm not a hot mess."

"Okay, then, you're a very warm one. And no, I won't pretend to be your girlfriend because you don't need to be in a relationship to prove you've moved on." She flitted a hand between Alex and Bridget. "Besides, there's no way I'm stepping in the middle of that unresolved tension."

Alex tossed a rag at her. "Shut up."

Bridget laughed as Benny tried to sit on her lap in the booth. It was a tight squeeze. "Okay, boy, I'm not sure this is going to work." She stopped laughing when she caught sight of Jordan Chambers approaching their table. *Oh, shit.*

"Hi," Jordan said. She stuck her hand out to Max. "I'm Jordan."

Max smiled and introduced himself.

"Bridget, I thought you and Max might want to join us, catch up a little."

Oh. Unexpected. Bridget raised her eyebrows at Max in a silent question, and he shrugged. "Okay, that'd be great, actually."

"Cool. We're over here."

Benny hopped down, letting Bridget and Max follow Jordan to a booth where Lu Salazar and Owen Kim were seated. Owen wore a welcoming smile, and with one hand, he gently rocked a baby in a stroller, but Lu had her arms crossed over her chest.

"My mom told me about your wedding, but I have must have missed this development. Congratulations," Bridget said to Owen and Jordan, indicating the stroller.

"Thanks," Owen said.

"Her name's Keiko," Jordan added.

"Well, she's adorable," Max said. "How old?"

"Twenty-one weeks," Owen said, clearly pleased as punch.

Jordan offered a patient smile. "In adult time, that's five months."

"Oh, yeah. Sometimes I forget not everyone speaks the language of childcare." He unclicked Keiko's straps. "Want to hold her?"

"Oh, um...sure?" Bridget answered, because this felt like a peace offering of sorts.

She sat in the chair Jordan had pulled over and took the little girl into her arms. Keiko had her dad's dark hair, but beyond that, Bridget couldn't tell which parent she took after more. She was definitely a cutie, though.

"Hello, sweets," she said. "I'm Bridget, and this is Max, and it's very nice to meet you."

For a few seconds, Keiko simply stared at her. Then she touched Bridget's cheek and laughed, a silly baby laugh that made Bridget chuckle, too.

"So, how long are you here?" Owen asked.

"Not sure yet," Bridget said. "It depends on…things." She couldn't help but glance at the bar, where Alex was talking to another bartender, but she quickly reverted her attention to Keiko, who was looking up at her with big brown eyes. Bridget booped her nose.

"Oh, yeah. 'Things,'" Lu said.

Bridget sipped her beer. Alex hadn't even wanted to *look* at her, and Lu, at least, didn't seem to want her here either. "Look, guys," she said, "we don't have to do this if you don't really want to, but…I am sorry that I lost contact with all of you. What happened between me and Alex was about me and Alex, but I never meant for you to have to choose sides."

"Well, you made us," Jordan said gently, "whether you meant to or not."

"Maybe we can start over," Bridget said. "I really have missed you."

"And Bridget's told me so much about you," Max added. "I'd love to get to know you all."

Bridget shot him a grateful smile, but it faded with Lu's next words.

"You can't miss people you've forgotten about," she said.

"Lu," Bridget said, a pleading tone in her voice, "I didn't forget about you. I thought you didn't want to speak to me. It seems I was right."

Jordan frowned. "I think what Lu means is that staying away for all these years made us feel cast aside. It looks like you went off to become this big star and then you forgot all about where you grew up."

Bridget blushed. She'd never meant to do that. Why couldn't everyone see that she hadn't come home because she couldn't face what she'd done, what she'd left behind?

"Yeah," Lu said, nodding. "Like, do you even know what's going on? Do you know that the Weylands' house burned down a couple years ago?

Or that the library had to completely tear down and rebuild because they found asbestos? Do you know that the elementary teachers are close to striking because they haven't had a raise in a decade?"

Bridget forced her knee to stop jiggling. "Well, okay, I'm obviously not up-to-date on town happenings. What can I do?"

Lu rolled her eyes. "Typical celebrity. She expects us to do all the work for her so she can throw some money around and be done with it."

"No, Lu, give her a chance. She's trying," Jordan said.

"The school building needs a new roof," Owen said. "We've been raising money for almost a year now, and we're still only halfway to our goal."

"Okay." Bridget tightened her hold on her glass. If she suggested paying for the roof, Lu would laugh at her. But she *could* offer to help with fundraising.

"Actually, if you're serious about wanting to give back to the community," Jordan said, lifting a finger, "I have an idea. Riley runs a nonprofit that builds houses for homeless and low-income families."

"Oh, yeah," Owen said. "Saturday mornings are big volunteer days, and I know she could use some extra hands tomorrow."

"That sounds like fun," Bridget said. "Max?"

He grinned. "Let's build some houses."

Chapter Three

Then

Alex rested her hands on Bridget's waist, the touch settling the tremor in them. Bridget was a bridesmaid in her brother's wedding, and the red sari she wore was modestly gorgeous. The whole day, Alex had been on the sidelines, a close friend of the groom's family but not involved in the ceremony. And the whole day, she'd been longing to touch Bridget, to be close to her, to step into her space, and let the world around them fade into nothing.

Now that she was here, even the feel of fabric-covered hips was enough to set her heart racing. She wanted and wanted and wanted, but forced herself to slow. She pulled Bridget closer, eliminating what little distance separated them. Her heart jumped when Bridget chuckled, breath warm against her neck.

They could have this one day, *would* have this one day. They'd find a venue in the countryside with a sturdy barn and an overgrown field of wildflowers, and they'd invite all the people they cared about, and they'd pledge to love each other for all eternity.

Bridget smelled like pomegranates and spice. Alex was heady with it.

"Are you all right?" Bridget asked, voice soft against the thumping music and the swirling conversations. Alex felt the question, saw it form on Bridget's lips, more than she heard it. "You've been really quiet."

Had she? Her mind had been so loud that she hadn't noticed. In an effort to ground herself, she swiped her thumb along the small of Bridget's back. "Just thinking."

Bridget smiled, tongue poking through her teeth. "Always thinking. You ever think about how your head might want a rest? It *is* a party, after all."

Smiling, Alex shook her head.

"Then tell me what you're thinking about."

In Portuguese, Alex whispered, "*I'm thinking about how much I want to marry you.*" Her lips slipped against Bridget's earlobe.

"What language was that?" Bridget asked, giggling. "Italian?"

Alex shook her head. "Portuguese."

"Ah. And what did you say?"

Alex swallowed thickly. Despite the blood rushing through her like it was rocket fuel, a new tranquility settled over her. She'd always kind of imagined love as a great unstoppable force, something that thrilled you and excited you until you were no longer capable of thinking clearly. But it wasn't that at all. It was a blanket that settled over you as you were tucked in safely and soundly for a good night's rest. It was standing in the eye of a hurricane. Maybe nothing around you made sense, but the fullness of your heart sure did.

"I'll tell you when you're not so tipsy," she said.

Bridget bopped her forefinger against Alex's nose. "Not fair."

"You won't even remember this in the morning."

"Oh, Alex," Bridget sighed, "I remember everything about you."

Alex's breath caught. "I love you," she murmured, feeling her heart fall into rhythm with the confession.

She'd said it so many times. Bridget had always made it a priority—in random texts, whispered as they were falling asleep, in sticky notes left in lunch bags. She said she did it to make sure Alex didn't forget. Like Alex could ever forget the surge of happiness that accompanied each utterance. Bridget made it a priority, and so had Alex. She'd said it so many times, but this time felt different.

Bridget stopped swaying to the music to look Alex full in the eye. Even in the dim lantern light, Bridget's eyes were a fantastic blue. Then, deliberately—as if she also knew the words were different this time for some reason that hung in the air and yet remained elusive—Bridget leaned forward. A soft groan escaped Alex's throat as she sank into the kiss. Not their first, not by a long shot, but *somehow*, it was different.

Bridget tasted like champagne.

She tasted like home.

Now

Alex cursed under her breath when she pulled up to the building site and saw Bridget and Riley up on the roof. That wasn't going to end well. Bridget had probably never picked up a hammer before, let alone installed a roof. It was dangerous. She could fall. Imagine the bad press for the town if they let America's Pop Princess fall off a fucking roof.

Alex grabbed her tea and Riley's coffee, exited her truck, and skirted around the volunteers on the ground, Max among them.

"Hey, Riley," she called.

Riley looked up. "Where's my coffee?"

Alex held up the to-go cups. "Right here. Now get down here. I want to talk to you."

Riley said something to Bridget, who laughed and nodded, before climbing down the ladder. She took the proffered cup and sipped. "Now, what's got your panties all in a twist?"

Alex frowned.

"I can't see your glare when you're wearing those sunglasses, you know."

Alex pushed them to the top of her head. "Stop being an ass. She shouldn't be up there."

"Why not? She's an adult."

"She's a first-time volunteer. That's a liability issue."

Riley turned toward the roof and shouted, "Hey, Bridget! Alex thinks you're too famous to be on the roof!"

"Come on, Lex," Bridget called down. "All the things we've done on rooftops? I've got good balance."

Riley snickered.

Alex pushed her in the shoulder.

"Okay, Al," Riley said, "I'm going to cut you some slack because you brought me this delicious coffee, but I don't really appreciate your insinuation that I'm not careful. In the five years I've been running this, not one person has so much as bashed their thumb with a hammer."

Alex shifted her weight onto her right foot. "I know."

"Good."

"I'm sorry."

"I know." Riley's expression softened. "You going to chill now?"

"Maybe."

"Better than nothing, I guess."

"You know your way around a roof. You could go up and help her out."

"No, I…" Alex looked around. "I'll find something else to do."

"Whatever. You look hot today. I bet she appreciates that."

Alex tugged self-consciously at her vest. "Shut up. I always look hot."

"Damn right," Riley said, laughing. "Now go make yourself useful."

Alex grumbled as Riley climbed the ladder again. She accidentally met Bridget's gaze. She froze for a moment because the look on Bridget's face was thoroughly unexpected—sadness tinged with…affection? That couldn't be right.

Turning away, Alex forced her mind to go blank. There was work to be done.

Bridget unwrapped her sandwich, then turned to Max. "Having fun yet?"

Beside her, Max nodded. "Oh, yeah. I might be an artsy boy, but I know my way around power tools."

Chuckling, she looked around. She and Max sat on the ground in a wide circle of adult volunteers who seemed too nervous to talk to her. A huddle of college kids here for volunteer hours sprawled on the grass nearby, tossing bits of bread at each other. Alex and Riley sat on the front steps of the house. Never had sixty feet felt so much like opposite ends of the world. Bridget let out a long breath, shoulders slumping.

Max stole a chip from her bag.

She jerked out of her daze to slap him on the hand. "Hey."

"You snooze, you lose, Cal."

Bridget scoffed.

"You should go talk to her."

"Like that turned out well last night."

"'If at first you don't succeed, try, try, try again.' William Edward Hickson."

"You're a nerd, Max."

"Yeah, a nerd who's helping you get your girl back." His smile turned mischievous. "Maybe *I* should go over there and talk to her." He stood up.

She grasped his elbow and dragged him back down to the ground. "Maybe you should sit your ass down and think again."

He collapsed in a fit of laughter.

"Ugh, this isn't funny." She scrubbed her face with her hands, and when she opened her eyes again, she caught Alex staring before quickly averting her gaze. Something clenched in Bridget's chest, squeezed until she almost couldn't breathe. Max was right. Obviously Alex wasn't going to be the one to make a move.

He gave her knee a squeeze. "Is that you changing your mind?"

She tightened her ponytail and brushed stray hair behind her ears. "I just… I'm never going to get closure if I can't get her to at least speak to me. Right?"

"Mm-hmm. I mean, what could it hurt?"

It could hurt a lot, actually. It could destroy everything. But hadn't she already done that five years ago?

She stood and walked straight toward Alex and Riley, her heart fluttering more with each step. Alex looked amazing, as usual. Her outfit—boots, jeans, gray Henley, black vest—was almost exactly what she used to wear on the camping trips they used to take. Bridget smiled at the memories. Those were some *good* trips.

"Hey, Bridget," Riley said. "What's up? Need some more Gatorade?"

That was when Bridget realized she'd been standing in front of them for a good few seconds, staring without saying a word. "Oh, um…I thought I could talk to Alex for a minute. If that's okay with Alex, of course."

Off a small nod from Alex, Riley got up. She touched Bridget's shoulder as she walked away. As soon as she was out of earshot, the look on Alex's face told Bridget this might have been a mistake. Still, she steeled herself and took a seat on the steps.

Breathe, Callahan. Breathe.

She hadn't been this close to Alex in years. This proximity used to be so normal. Even before they'd started dating, their friendship was all handholding and chaste touches and a primal desire just to be near the only other person on the planet who *got* them. The years had been good to Alex, matured her features so that her teenage attractiveness had become straight-up adult beauty. Or perhaps it was the absence that made Bridget appreciate the plump lips, the bottomless brown eyes, the long nose all the more. And, oh, God, her hair. Bridget wanted to bury her fingers in those curls and never look back.

Alex busied herself with retying her boots, clearly not keen to start the conversation. She hadn't moved away, though. That was cause to be hopeful, right?

"Alex..." For a heartbeat, Bridget could pretend nothing had changed. Despite the uncrossable chasm between them, they were tied together by broken promises and broken hearts. That had to count for something.

"I've missed you," were the words that slipped from her lips. Then she closed her eyes because that was the worst thing to say, something she had no right to say anymore.

"Look," Alex said, "I can't object to you coming back here since it's your hometown, too, but that doesn't mean this is eas—" She took a deep breath. "Maybe we should just stay out of each other's way."

She moved to stand, but Bridget put a hand on her knee. Alex glared, the expression foreign and unsettling.

Bridget jerked her hand away. "I'll respect that, Alex. I will. But I think a semblance of closure could do us some good." She swallowed thickly. "One conversation. A few minutes. That's all I'm asking for."

Alex squinted out into the fall sunshine.

Bridget felt suspended from a string, like Alex's next words were the only thing keeping her from plunging to her death.

"Closure," Alex said with a quiet, mirthless chuckle. Then she stood and brushed off her pants, and just like that, Alex was walking away from her.

If there was any proof that karma existed, this was it right here—the worst act Bridget had ever committed now turned against her every time they interacted.

Bridget chased her. Wasn't that her fate now? To right her wrongs, to fix everything she'd broken or to die trying. Alex wasn't like her. She was quiet, all of her emotions roiling unseen beneath the surface. She needed time to process things. Bridget knew this, and yet it still felt like a slap in the face. Still felt like punishment.

"Hey!" Bridget called after her. "Alex!" In her haste, she smacked into a stack of wooden planks, and her foot twisted around. Pain lanced through her toes and ankle, and she fell forward hard onto the grass before a sturdy pair of arms latched around her and gently turned her onto her back. She groaned, not wanting to look and see who it was.

"Are you all right?" Riley asked, voice too far away to be the person holding her.

Bridget opened her eyes.

Alex. Alex was there, on a knee, arms scooped up under Bridget.

Heat crept up Bridget's neck. Her cheeks were surely splotchy with it. Fantastic. "I'm fine. I'm fine."

She tried to push to her feet, only to have Alex lift her upright. After the barely there conversation they'd just had, gentleness was the last thing Bridget expected, but Alex allowed Bridget to lean on her as she found her footing.

Which wasn't too easy, given that her ankle gave out as soon as she put weight on it. Once again, Alex was there with an arm beneath her shoulders.

Max came running over. "What's going on? Bridge, are you all right?"

"Mostly," she said. "I think I just twisted my ankle. A little rest, a pack of ice, and I'll be fine."

"No, you should go get it checked out," Riley said. "Come on. I'll take you."

"No, I'll do it," Alex said.

All three heads swiveled toward her.

Alex shrugged. "That way, you don't have to call off the day for the other volunteers."

Riley looked nonplussed for a second before asking Bridget, "Is that okay with you?"

Bridget nodded. At least twelve minutes in the car with the woman who kept avoiding her? Yeah, that was more than okay.

"Okay. Alex, call me later," Riley said, "especially if it's anything more than a twist."

"Sure," Alex said.

"Want me to come along?" Max asked.

"No," Bridget said. "It's probably nothing, anyway. I'll meet you back home."

"Okay."

Alex, one arm under Bridget's, hand splayed against her back, dipped her knees a few inches to make Bridget more comfortable. After a short trek to the curb, they paused beside a relatively new black truck.

Alex popped the lock and pulled open the passenger door. "It's a bit of a step. Sorry."

Alex helped her up into the cab, even pulled out the seatbelt to hand over and closed the door for her. Bridget watched Alex move around the front of the truck and get in.

"So, you got a new truck," Bridget said.

"Mm-hmm," Alex agreed as she started the engine and pulled away.

"Cool."

"Comes in handy."

Bridget worried her bottom lip. Honestly, why had Alex even volunteered for this if she didn't want to? And, despite her kindness in helping Bridget into the truck, her short responses and inability to make eye contact showed her cards. She clearly didn't want to be here. Sore at the thought, Bridget said, "You didn't have to drive me, you know. Max would have done it."

Alex's voice was flat, unreadable when she said, "Max doesn't know the way."

It would have been a flimsy excuse even before the age of GPS; Bridget knew this town well enough to give directions. So maybe Alex *did* want to be here, just didn't want to show it. Bridget fidgeted with the hem of her sweatshirt, and by the time she thought of something suitable to say, they were pulling into the parking lot of the doctor's office.

Dr. Jane Kozlow was six years older than the last time Bridget had seen her, but her take-no-shit face hadn't aged a day. Bridget lowered her shoulders in an attempt to shrink into the exam table.

Jane addressed Alex, who stood uncomfortably in the doorway. "Alex, thank you for bringing her, but I'd like to examine the patient in private."

"Of course. I'll be in the waiting room."

Bridget licked her lips as her gaze followed Alex's ass, but her fantasizing was disrupted by Jane smacking her in the head. "Ow! What was that for?"

Jane crossed her arms. Who knew a sixty-year-old sitting on a swivel stool could be so intimidating? "Level with me, Bridget."

The paper rattled as Bridget tightened her grip on the exam table.

"Scale of one to ten. How badly does your ankle *actually* hurt?"

Bridget squished her nose up. "Uh…point-five?"

Jane nodded. "That's what I thought. Now, would you care to elaborate on why you're wasting my time by faking an injury when I could be dealing with real emergencies?"

"I'm not faking. It hurt for a bit, but the pain pretty much faded on the ride over. And come on, Doc. The only emergencies in this town are the fights over at the bingo hall."

"You'd be surprised how vicious people can get over that game. Count yourself lucky if you've gotten out of there with only minor scrapes and bruises." Jane tapped her pen against the clipboard. "And don't change the subject."

Bridget let out a breath and, along with it, a fraction of the tension in her body. "I'm sorry I took up your time, but I did it for love, and—"

"Oh, well, if it's for love…"

"That makes it okay?"

"Of course not!" Jane said. She straightened the lapels of her white coat. "I expect tickets for your next concert in Pittsburgh for my grandchildren."

Unexpected, but easy enough. "Done."

Jane gestured. "Continue."

"Alex won't speak to me. She'll barely even look at me. But when I fell, she was right there, like she hasn't been able to rid herself of that instinct to protect me. And, starved for any sort of attention from her, I got carried away in the moment." Bridget frowned.

Jane narrowed her eyes. "You're very dramatic. Has anyone ever told you that?"

"Many times. Unfortunately, drama kind of comes with the territory," Bridget said, unsure if she was referring to being a pop star or the tension with her ex.

"So you came home to get her back?"

'Getting her back' would require Alex wanting her, too. Bridget would be content with much less. "It factored into the decision."

Jane's gaze lost focus for a moment, as if she were lost in memories. She sighed. "Then I suppose I'll go along with this little charade of yours."

"Thank you!"

"If you hurt her again, the only head that will roll will be yours. Do you understand?"

"Yes, Doctor."

"And don't forget those tickets."

Bridget eased onto her feet. "I won't. I promise. Thank you."

Hopping slightly, Bridget followed Jane back to the waiting room, where Alex sat sullenly in a chair, playing with the zipper of her vest.

"Well, she'll live," Jane said.

Alex nodded and stood. "Good."

To Bridget, the doctor added, "But you need to keep weight off your foot for a day or two. And you'll need to ice and elevate it the rest of the day. You'll see her home, Alex?"

Alex's jaw jumped. Bridget did her best to seem in need of aid without being a total damsel in distress, but she was sure, just from her ex-girlfriend's tense posture, that Alex would say no.

After a moment, though, Alex waved toward the door. "Come on, then."

Relief and anticipation were quickly followed by dread. Because the trip to the doctor's office had been an awfully quiet one. The thrill that went through her when Alex slipped an arm under hers, though—that was worth all the dread in the world.

Alex gripped the steering wheel hard. Catching Bridget had been nothing more than a reaction, but it had cost her. Five years of fighting it, and five hours had reduced her to an emotional puddle whose first instinct, upon seeing Bridget stub her toe, was to catch her like this was some heteronormative rom-com.

She could beat this. Bridget would be gone soon enough. Her life would return to normal. In a few days, she wouldn't have to worry about Bridget's presence stirring up old emotions.

Alex flipped on the radio. Distractions were good. The rock song that was playing came to an end, only to be replaced by Bridget's latest single. Of fucking course. Inescapable.

Bridget shut off the music. "Alex, listen, I know you hate me, but I—"

"I don't hate you," Alex said softly.

"What?"

"I said I don't hate you." She swallowed her emotions. It was tougher with Bridget in the passenger seat, but she'd had years of practice. "It'd be easier to hate you if you were terrible."

That got a smile from Bridget. "You want me to be terrible? Okay, what do you call a belt made out of a watch?" She paused expectantly. "A waist of time!"

Alex groaned. If she weren't driving, she'd cover her eyes with a palm. "That was awful."

Bridget laughed. "You love it."

She did, but it was a residual sort of love, the thing she never learned to stop loving because she was so busy forgetting Bridget's eyes and her voice and her thoughtfulness.

"So," Bridget began, twisting her fingers together, "I know we should find a better time to talk, but I thought...I thought maybe we could try to be friends?"

Alex tightened her jaw to keep from replying right away. *Absolutely not* was her kneejerk reaction. Because that was what she did. React and hold grudges and squirrel herself away so no one could make her feel anything. When you were alone, the only person who could hurt you was yourself.

She stayed silent for three more blocks, long enough to prompt Bridget into talking again. "Or not. That's fine, too. That's...totally fine. But, you know, we should talk. At some point."

They reached Bridget's house a block later. Alex pulled the truck into the driveway next to Evelyn's car. She hopped out, jogged around the truck, and had the passenger door open before Bridget even got her seatbelt off.

Bridget hesitated before letting Alex get an arm under her and help her hobble to the front door. The walk was short, blessedly so, because holding Bridget was...

Douse those flames. Build those walls.

Mrs. Callahan opened the door. "Oh, honey, Max called and told me what happened. Are you all right?"

"Yeah, Mom, I'm fine," Bridget said, as Alex helped her inside and onto the couch.

"Thank you so much for taking care of her, Alex," Mrs. Callahan said.

"Not a problem, Mrs. C."

"Would you like to stay? I'm making lasagna for dinner."

"Thank you, but I can't today."

"Mom," Bridget said, making a little *go away* motion with her head.

"Of course, dear. Alex, thanks again for being such an upstanding young woman."

Alex smiled. Mrs. Callahan was laying it on thick today.

Bridget perched on the couch, seemingly content to stare at Alex without a word.

Alex stuffed her hands in the pockets of her vest. She cleared her throat. "So, um, friends. You said you wanted us to try to be friends."

A small, tentative smile appeared on Bridget's lips. "Yeah, I did. What do you think?"

Five years was a long time to analyze flaws, and Alex knew she had them. Lots. But she'd never get better if she didn't own up to them. Besides, all she could think about was her dad's face if he knew how thoroughly she'd shut Bridget out. Bridget had been like a second daughter to him, and he'd always advocated forgiveness.

Too bad she wasn't that good a person.

"Yeah... I don't think so."

Chapter Four

Then

THE SIMPLE FACT WAS, THE summer was turning out to be freakishly hot and, as poor college students, she and Alex couldn't afford an apartment with air conditioning. That was why every single window was open, letting in the noise of cars and partiers from the street. That was why every single ceiling fan was at full speed and they'd borrowed standing fans from her family. That was why they'd been living on takeout and peanut butter and jelly sandwiches for the past week, because they didn't want to heat up the apartment by using the oven.

It wasn't the reason they hadn't had sex in four days, though.

Not that Bridget was counting.

But it was almost the end of the summer, almost the beginning of their senior year, and Alex had spent the past three months consumed by her internship. Bridget didn't blame her, exactly, but she had imagined this time would be theirs. Instead, she was wasting away as a barista at the local coffee shop while Alex worked insanely long hours for minimum wage and the promise of a recommendation letter.

She wasn't going to waste a Friday night, though. With plans to meet their friends for dinner and dancing, she left Alex hunched over her laptop and called over her shoulder, "I'm taking a shower." A cold one to combat the heat.

She dressed in red shorts that barely covered her ass, a white ribbed tank top, and a loose, short-sleeved plaid shirt she could take off if it got too hot. Alex barely looked up when Bridget said goodnight and told her not to wait up.

Bridget tried not to let it sting, but it distracted her all through dinner. When they got to the club afterward, she downed two shots of vodka in the same number of minutes and hit the dance floor, ignoring her friends' concerned looks. She didn't want to tell them about Alex ignoring her, even if it wasn't intentional. All she wanted to do was lose herself in the music and maybe, if she let her hair down, a new dance partner.

Five drinks into the night, she'd found multiple. Her current was a jock, his beefy arms almost busting through his white T-shirt. When the pulsing beat of the song ended, someone pulled her away from him.

"Hey, hey, hey," Bridget said.

"Time to go home, princess," Jordan said.

"But I'm not done dancing," Bridget whined.

Lu appeared at her other side. "Yes, you are. Trust me—you'll thank us in the morning."

As they led her out of the club, Bridget asked, "Can I at least stay with you two tonight?"

Tipsy as she was, Bridget didn't miss the weighted glance between her friends.

"Trouble in paradise?" Jordan asked nonchalantly.

Bridget grumbled. She wanted to get into it, but she didn't want to get into it. She didn't know what she wanted. Besides ten hours of uninterrupted sleep.

It wasn't until they'd made it back to the apartment and all collapsed in the living room that Jordan ventured, "Does this have anything to do with Alex being busy tonight?"

Bridget threw up her hands. "It's Friday night! And she's doing work! For her internship. That pays her a pittance. This was supposed to be our summer."

Lu reached an arm around her shoulders. "Oh, Bridge, I know, but this is really important for her career."

"It'll be better in the long run," Jordan said. "Just make the time you do get to be together special."

Bridget sighed into Lu's shoulder. They had good points, but her brain was foggy and she didn't have the energy to talk about it anymore.

In the morning, though her hangover was rather staggering, she stumbled back home at a very respectable ten AM only to find Alex still asleep.

Bridget brushed her teeth for the second time that morning before changing into one of Alex's old T-shirts and getting into bed with her.

Stirring, Alex flipped to face her. "Hey. Thanks for the text last night."

"Mm-hmm." Despite her hurt feelings, she would always let Alex know where she was. And even though she was still a little bit upset, Alex looked so darn adorable with her messy curls and bleary brown eyes that Bridget pressed a soft kiss to her lips.

Alex hummed in contentment and closed her eyes. "What do you want to do today?"

Bridget tucked herself close to Alex, one arm thrown over her waist. "I thought you had a lot of work this weekend."

"I finished it last night."

Bridget raised an eyebrow even though Alex couldn't see. "How late were you up?"

"Late," Alex said.

"You had all weekend. Why'd you stay up?"

Alex buried her nose in the crook of Bridget's neck, nuzzling the skin there. "Because I've been working nonstop this summer, and that's not fair to you."

"Alex…" Bridget dropped a kiss against Alex's hair. "I haven't been that fair to you, either."

Alex inhaled deeply and entwined their fingers. "It might take me a while to find a good balance, but I promise I'll keep trying."

And they fell asleep in each other's arms.

Now

Arms crossed, Alex sat at the end of the bench in their lane. The bowling alley smelled like popcorn and fried food, and the speakers were piping '90s pop songs. On any other night, with any other company, she'd be having a grand old time. Tonight, though, she'd been suckered into a night out.

Which would have been fine had her friends not conveniently forgotten to tell her they'd invited Bridget and Max, too.

They probably had bets on how long she'd last without insulting someone or downright escaping.

Because that second option seemed more sensible, she was almost out of her seat when Lu, stationed by the computer screen, turned and said, "You're up, Al."

Alex shook herself back into the real world. The rest of their group—Lu, Owen, Jordan, Max, and Bridget—all looked at her expectantly. She dragged herself over to the rack and sifted through, looking for a lightweight ball. She could use a heavier one, but they'd signed up for three games, and she was too competitive to allow flagging in the third.

"Oh, hey!" Bridget grabbed an orange ball from a nearby rack and held it out. "This is only six pounds."

Alex took it, the brush of Bridget's hands against hers sending her right back into the land of the dazed. "Thanks."

Bridget grinned. "No problem," she said, retaking her seat beside Max.

Alex stepped onto the pine ledge. She took a deep breath. She could deal with being in the same room as her ex. No big deal at all.

Her throw split the pins, leaving the seven and the ten. Despite trying her best to add some spin, she hit only one of the remaining pins with her second throw. Her friends clapped anyway.

"You'll get that split next time," Jordan assured her.

"I'm crap at splits, and you know it," Alex said, smiling nevertheless.

As Max got up to bowl his frame, Owen said, "So, some mysterious benefactor paid for the school roof out of the blue. You wouldn't happen to know anything about that, would you, Bridget?"

"Me? No." Bridget said, much too nonchalantly, then clapped wildly when Max got a strike.

That was the Bridget Alex knew. Generous, but embarrassed by attention for it.

"Huh," Owen said, clearly not convinced.

An unfamiliar tug in her chest, Alex wasn't sure why she said, "Could have been one of those rich old coots who live on top of the hill."

"Yeah," Lu scoffed, picking out a ball. "You know how they like to die and leave barrels of money to the town."

Owen frowned, but Jordan rested a hand on his shoulder and gave it a squeeze. Then she turned to Bridget. "How's your ankle feeling?"

Alex huffed, annoyed with herself. That little display of kindness hadn't been in her plans.

"I had to stay off it the rest of the day and ice it on and off on Sunday," Bridget said, "but it's back to normal now. Thanks for asking." She jumped up. "Who's up for snacks? I'll get the first round!"

Jordan motioned her back into her seat. "No, seriously, you paid for our games and shoes. You can at least let us get the pizza and beer."

Max half-smiled and tugged a frowning Bridget gently back to the bench, where she pulled one knee against her chest. Something unspoken passed between them, eliciting a sting of jealousy from Alex. She squashed it immediately.

"Any special requests?" Jordan asked.

Alex lifted a hand. "I'll take some —"

"Yes, mozzarella sticks for you," Jordan cut her off. "We already know."

"You know you own a bar, right?" Lu teased. "You can get bar food anytime."

"Oh, don't take her fried cheese away from her," Owen said. "She wouldn't be Alex if she weren't completely predictable."

"Come on, guys," Bridget said, locking gazes with Alex. "She's not *completely* predictable. Besides, even if she is, who cares? She's steady. Steady is good."

"At least someone appreciates me," Alex said with a nod at Bridget. "For your efforts, you get a mozzarella stick." *God, were they flirting?*

Bridget lifted a hand to her heart and dipped her chin. "I'm honored."

For a second, it was almost easy. To forget the pain they'd caused each other in the past. To forget the chasm gaping between them now.

Owen stood. "I'll come with you, Jor."

Also easy to snap out of it.

As Jordan and Owen walked away, Lu made a fake-disgusted face, drawing a laugh from Max. "Sometimes they give me heartburn," she said. "Single suits me just fine, thank you."

"Same," Max said.

"Oh?" Lu asked. She flicked a hand between him and Bridget. "So... you two..."

"No," Bridget said quickly. "Never."

"Gee, thanks," Max said.

Alex didn't miss Lu's pointed look her way, but she ignored it to focus on Bridget, whose face had reddened. How many times had she been asked that question by the press?

Bridget smacked Max in the ribs. "You know what I meant."

Her gaze slid past him to catch Alex staring. Not staring. Just looking. There was no harm in that.

Still, she looked away and tossed a wadded-up gum wrapper at Lu's head. "Whose turn is it? You're slacking over there."

Lu stuck out her tongue. "Bridget's up."

"Oh, sorry!" Bridget moved to select a bowling ball. Her skinny jeans hugged everything just right, from hips to thighs to calves.

When Alex forced her eyes away, Max was regarding her with a curious expression, one eyebrow lifted.

She returned his look. "What?"

He shrugged. "Nothing." But a smile lingered on his lips.

Bridget's throw was perfect, knocking down all ten pins. "Yes!" She whirled around, clapping and grinning. "Did you see that?" She high-fived Lu and Max before flopping back onto the bench.

"Nice one," Lu said. Owen was up next, but he and Jordan hadn't returned yet.

The conversation lagged. Alex untied and retied the laces of her bowling shoes. It wasn't awkward, exactly. Just…sad. *She* was sad. Overhead, the music changed to a Mariah Carey song, one that pulled up long-ignored memories of middle school dances and sleepovers.

Bridget squealed in delight, jumping up to dance right there in the middle of the bowling alley. "Lu! Alex! Do you remember this? This was our jam!"

Max, laughing, allowed her to pull him to his feet. His fluid movements matched hers. Lu rolled her eyes, but even she started wiggling in her seat.

"Come on! For old times' sake!" Bridget said to Alex, reaching out a hand.

"This is crazy," Alex said in an effort to stop her smile.

"What, having fun? You never did like dancing."

No, she never had. She was more an observer, a wallflower, though Bridget had a way of letting her forget that.

Bridget leaned forward, scrunched her eyes shut, and sang a few lines enthusiastically—exactly like she used to do in their bedrooms on weekend nights. Alex erupted in laughter. Maybe Bridget hadn't changed so much at all. Was that a good thing or a bad thing?

"I can't dance," she protested, a weary refrain from a past life, even as she allowed Bridget to pull her to her feet.

"Are you moving? Is there music on?" Bridget asked. "Then you're dancing."

And then it was all shouting lyrics in each other's faces and hopping around and never, ever letting their hands break apart. For one brief, shining moment, being adult enough to be friends seemed possible.

Owen and Jordan's return broke the spell. Their arms were laden with food, and Lu and Max beelined for it. Alex retook her seat, leaving Bridget to finish out the song alone. Jordan handed her a cup of beer. Throat dry, she gulped down a third of it and blamed her shortness of breath on the dancing.

After washing her hands, Bridget splashed water on her face and studied herself in the bathroom mirror. Being so close to Alex was both thrilling and agonizing. She wanted to jump right back in with both feet, and sometimes, it seemed like Alex was right there on the edge with her. Then Alex's eyes would go cold and she'd step away and they'd be back to barely speaking. Bridget splashed her face again, toweled it off, and left the bathroom.

And walked right into a group of giggling teenage girls, phones out, whispering among themselves, awkwardly adorable. Faced with her idol at their age, Bridget would have been much more of a mess.

"Hi," she said, setting off another round of high-pitched laughter.

"We love you, Bridget! Can we get a picture with you?" a redhead said.

"Of course!" Bridget shuffled the group away from the bathroom door and in front of a rack of bowling balls.

She threw her arms around the two on either side of her as the brunette at the end of their group took half a dozen selfies. She spent the next ten minutes chatting with the girls, taking individual photos with each of them, and signing everything from phone cases to forearms.

"Tag me in those, okay?" she said when they were through, evoking giant grins.

Four of the girls hurried back to their lane. The smallest, Jenny, lingered, wringing her hands.

"You all right?" Bridget asked.

Jenny nodded. "I have a question actually."

"Shoot."

Jenny hesitated before she leaned closer and whispered, "I was just wondering…how did you know you liked girls too?"

Bridget smiled. She'd been there. Been confused, been told she was wrong. For months, she'd agonized over her attraction to girls, especially to Alex, her *best friend*. It had seemed like a sacred bond she could never touch. But speaking up, telling the truth, kissing Alex that first time had led to years of bliss. "Who's the girl?"

Jenny pointed discreetly in the direction of her friends. "Mallory."

"The tall one? With glasses?"

Jenny nodded eagerly, hardly able to tear her eyes away from her crush.

"Well, for me, it was kind of like that," Bridget said. "There was this girl I liked—*really* liked. In fact, she's right over there." She gestured to Alex, in line at the concession stand. "I'd known her for years, but suddenly, seeing her gave me butterflies, and every time we held hands, I wanted it to be as something more, and I couldn't stop thinking about what it'd be like to kiss her."

"That's how I feel, too. What did you do about it?"

"I was scared, mostly. So I kept it to myself for a long time. But then she kissed me right here." Bridget touched her cheek. "And I finally got the courage to kiss her for real. I'm not saying to do that, but it's okay if you don't figure it out right away. It's okay to spend time with her. It's okay if it takes a while to find the courage to tell her you like her."

Jenny smiled. "I think I can do that."

"Good. The important thing is to stop worrying so much. No one says you have to have it all figured out at fifteen. I'm almost twice your age, and I still don't have it figured out."

"Really?" Jenny twisted to look at Alex. "But I thought you said she liked you back."

Bridget's smile slid away with a familiar pang. "She did once. A long time ago, I made a mistake, but I'm trying to fix it now."

"I hope you can."

"And I hope Mallory has butterflies for you, too."

The group of teenagers called Jenny's name. "I'm up! Gotta go! Thanks, Bridget!" She threw her arms around Bridget's neck before running off to rejoin her group, high-fiving her crush like a pro.

Bridget forced her lungs to work properly. To be a teenager again, figuring out what the fluttering in her chest meant, figuring out why being with her best friend felt so damn good in so many ways. But she wasn't a teenager. And Alex wasn't her best friend anymore.

Alex leaned her elbows on the bar, waiting on two more pitchers of beer. Across the way, Bridget was deep in conversation with a teenage girl. This side of America's Sweetheart was truly sweet to see. Bridget always did love to put smiles on people's faces.

Max sidled up to her. "Figured you could use a hand."

"Two pitchers, two hands," she said, "but thanks."

Unfazed, he said, "A friend, then?"

The bartender placed the beer on the counter. Alex thanked him, took the pitchers, and turned away. "If you're here to talk about what I think you want to talk about, I'm not really interested."

"Oh, that's too bad. I loved the beer I had at your bar, and Jordan led me to believe I could get a tour of your brewery if I played my cards right."

A laugh slipped out. That was something she could do.

"Sure," she said. "Come by the bar during the day sometime next week, and I'll give you a tour."

Max grinned.

He seemed like a nice guy—caring, funny, kind. She was glad Bridget had him.

Chapter Five

Then

GIDDINESS AND EXHAUSTION WARRED WITHIN Bridget as the spray of the shower washed over her. The ceremony had been followed by lunch with their families and partying with their friends. And all four years of exhaustion were worth it now that they had diplomas. If college had been like treading water, she looked forward to knowing what it felt like to swim in the open sea.

After drying off, she threw on an oversized T-shirt and nothing else, toweled her hair, and ran her fingers through it. Then, heart thudding with happiness and desire, she walked into the bedroom.

Alex sat on her side of the bed, back against the headboard, a book propped on her knees, glasses on her nose. Something crystalized within Bridget. This was her future—being able to slip into bed beside a soft, caring woman. She'd thought about it, of course. She'd thought about it a lot over the last four years, but college had felt so temporary. It was so much more real now, like they weren't just playing at being adults anymore

Alex looked up, a smile forming on her lips.

Bridget crawled under the covers, gently took the book from Alex's lap, and moved to straddle her. Alex's hands came around her waist, her eyes holding so much affection that Bridget had to swallow down a lump in her throat. What they had was special, and she knew how lucky they were to have found each other so quickly, so effortlessly.

One hand threading into Alex's hair, she leaned down to kiss her. Everything about Alex was soft—from the give of her lips to the taste of tea on her tongue to the way she cradled Bridget. As their mouths moved together, Bridget's heart swelled. She felt so *safe* with Alex, so cherished and cared for.

As the kiss ended, she leaned her forehead against Alex's. "Hey," she murmured.

"Hey," Alex murmured back.

These moments—the ones where they didn't really have to speak, could simply enjoy being in each other's presence—were some of Bridget's favorites. She focused on the gentle puff of Alex's breath against her cheek, the splay of Alex's slender fingers against her back, the rapid rise and fall of Alex's chest. She couldn't decide if she wanted to live in this moment or bottle it up so she could carry it with her forever.

"Can you believe we made it?" Bridget said.

"Of course I can. We did it together," Alex said, slipping a hand under Bridget's shirt.

Her touch, though cool, set Bridget on fire. Bridget pushed up the hem of Alex's boxers and shifted so they were skin-on-skin. Alex's eyes narrowed. She scratched her nails over Bridget's lower back and leaned in to kiss Bridget's neck.

Alex had a way with her tongue, and Bridget's breath came in shudders at the heat from Alex's mouth and the answering heat growing in her own body. She threaded her fingers through Alex's hair. A breathy moan escaped her lips as Alex nibbled at her ear.

What she loved most about coming unraveled under Alex's touch was the consideration and the gentleness in it. This was her own personal heaven, one she got to experience every single day.

"This is the beginning of the rest of our lives," she breathed in Alex's ear.

"Mm. And what are we going to do with our newfound freedom?" Alex murmured, voice husky and low, as she dipped down to Bridget's collarbone.

Bridget, rocking against Alex, tightened her grip in her hair. Desire pulsed through her. "Oh, I've got plans for us," she said. She ran her thumb in circles over the nape of Alex's neck, making her shiver. "First, I'm going to make love to you until the only thing you can say is my name."

Alex huffed out a laugh. She pulled away to look at Bridget, a challenge in her eye. "Are you sure about that?"

Before Bridget could question it, could make sure Alex wanted to do this tonight, Alex flipped them over. Her weight, solid and sexy, only increased Bridget's longing, as did the knee she slipped between Bridget's thighs.

"Alex," Bridget groaned, need dripping from her voice. In front of anyone else, it would have been embarrassing. But for Alex, she willingly laid herself bare; she knew Alex would take care of her.

Brown curls haloing her face, Alex grinned down at her. "I think you're going to have to wait your turn."

Now

Alex stood in front of the Callahans' door, a six-pack of beer in one hand and a bouquet of flowers from her back garden in the other. Once, she would've walked right in. Like a second daughter. She licked her lips, thinking of her grandmother's ring and how she almost *was* an actual second daughter.

After tucking the flowers under her arm, she wiped her sweaty palms off on her jeans, fixed the collar of her flannel shirt, and smoothed the front of her sweater. Only then did she knock.

Evelyn opened the door promptly, a wide smile on her face. "Alex!" She leaned in for a hug, noticing Alex's offerings as she pulled back. "Sweetie, I know you're stubborn about the knocking, but how many times have I told you that you don't have to bring anything?"

"Every week."

Evelyn led them inside. "And how many times have you brought something?"

Alex followed her into the foyer. "Every week."

Evelyn chuckled. "You're a lost cause, I'm afraid."

"So I've been told," Alex said. She held up the six-pack. "I thought you'd like to try the new brew."

"Oh, something new?" Marcus asked, poking his head in from the dining room. He rubbed his hands together before taking the carrier from her. "Excellent."

"You'll have to let me know what you think."

"Will do, kid."

Alex rolled her eyes as he disappeared into the dining room. She'd never needed to wish for siblings; Bridget's brothers had always seemed like her own.

"Everyone's out back," Evelyn said, tipping her head in that direction. "Maybe you want to join them."

Alex hesitated. Evelyn was one of her favorite people on the planet, but she couldn't give her what she wanted. Not right now, maybe not ever. She held up the bundle of flowers. "Actually, I should probably get these in water, so…"

A sad smile on her face, Evelyn nodded.

Alex knew where the vases were. She knew where practically everything in this house was, and every spot, every nook brought up a memory of simpler, better times. The sofa in the living room, where they'd spent countless weekend nights watching movies and, as they'd grown older, gotten a little handsy under blankets. The kitchen table, where a teenaged Bridget had patched up Alex's skinned knees after some boys pushed her off her bike.

Every other Sunday, Alex had been able to bury those memories just deep enough to get through family dinner.

She grabbed a plain vase from the bottom cabinet near the dishwasher and filled it up. Standing at the sink gave her a perfect view of the backyard. The backyard, where Bridget was pushing her nephew on the swing set. Before she could stop herself, she was thinking about where they'd be right now if they hadn't split.

Five years was a long time.

They'd be married, definitely. Would they be living in the city, close enough to drop by for family time every Sunday? Would they have had kids by now? Or at least be starting the long, arduous adoption process?

Bridget's hair shone in the autumn sunlight. Alex's breath came shakily. They could've had this. They could've had a life together, could've been *happy*, and Bridget just…left. She left like Alex meant nothing to her. Like it was the easiest decision in the world. Alex bit her bottom lip to keep her emotions in check.

Bridget, still pushing Dev, finally looked up.

Alex immediately looked down. The vase was overflowing.

Bridget's laugh died on her lips when she looked up. Alex was in the kitchen window, looking right back her.

"What's happening? Why is Alex…" She trailed off, made for the back door.

Ian grabbed her by the arm and gently spun her around. "Bridge, Bridge, Bridge. Just hang on a sec, okay?"

"What?" she asked. "What is it you're not telling me?"

"I'm sorry," Jaya soothed, her voice smooth and sincere. "I don't think any of us thought she'd come this week."

"This week?" Bridget repeated. She rounded on her brother and sister-in-law. "So, this happens *every* week? Why didn't you tell me?"

Ian, chagrined, rubbed the back of his neck. "We were trying to help."

"Both of you," Jaya clarified. "We were trying to help both of you in different ways."

"You're my family," Bridget said. "You're supposed to be on my side."

Jaya took her hand. "Bridget, sweetie, there are no sides."

"Yeah, just because we still love her doesn't mean we love you less or something," Ian said.

"She hasn't had anyone, not since her dad died," Jaya said, lightly squeezing Bridget's hand. "Don't ask us to abandon her."

Bridget swallowed thickly. Right. She couldn't begrudge Alex finding solace in the only semblance of family she had left. She swiped her hands under her eyes. "I'm not asking that. I just… You should have told me."

"Yeah, we should have," Ian said.

He folded her into his arms, and Jaya followed soon after. Dev and Arya barreled into their knees in an effort to join the group hug, drawing a wet chuckle from Bridget's lips.

"You're strong. You can do this," Jaya said.

Bridget wasn't so sure about that, but she followed them into the house anyway, the kids at their heels. She pulled the sleeves of her sweater over her hands, burrowed into the wool like it would hide her from Alex's radar. She'd performed at the Grammy Awards. She could certainly sit through an awkward dinner.

A glass of wine couldn't hurt, though. She headed to the kitchen to pour one and nearly bumped right into Alex, who held a glass in each hand.

"Sorry, sorry," Bridget said.

"It's okay," Alex said in that calm, measured way she had. It used to drive Bridget crazy, how Alex could be so stoic. She used to make a game of trying to get a rise out of her. Now, though, it just made her sad.

"I was just..." Bridget gestured into the kitchen. "Wine."

Alex held out a glass. "I was just bringing you one, actually."

"Oh, um, thanks." As she accepted, Bridget silently cursed the heat rising to her cheeks.

Alex brushed by her to take a seat at the dining room table. Max and Marcus already sat next to each other on one side, with Ian, Jaya, and Alex across from them. Her mom sat at the head of the table, and across from her, Arya and Dev sat together.

Which left the chair beside Max, the one across from Alex, for Bridget. She slipped into it and immediately took a gulp of wine. It was white and sweet, like she liked it. She never did get the taste for anything drier than Riesling. Did Alex remember that about her, or was it just a guess? Was it just what Alex happened to be drinking herself?

Max gave her knee a squeeze, a question in his half-smile. She nodded. She was all right.

After they said grace, Arya passed the bowl of bread to her. She took two slices. When she looked up, her eyes were drawn to Alex, who studied her plate intently. So once they were done passing food and Bridget's plate was piled with lasagna, roasted vegetables, and mashed potatoes, she let her gaze linger. Alex looked healthy, if not quite happy. And Bridget always did love her in flannel.

She forced air in and out of her lungs. This was all so...normal. Alex apparently came here for lunch every Sunday.

Every. Single. Week.

And her mom, Marcus, Ian, Jaya—none of them had ever breathed a word of it to her. But it was fine. It was fine because Bridget leaving didn't mean all the Callahans had to decamp. It didn't mean Alex had to lose everyone.

Alex deserved so much more than a coward like her, but that didn't stop a part of Bridget, the selfish part, from wanting this to be completely normal—*her* presence at the table, too. This was what their life could've been, if she had tried a bit harder instead of leaving when Alex needed her most. She could imagine sitting beside Alex, their knees brushing, letting her hand creep up Alex's thigh as Alex fought a grin. She could imagine Alex joking with Marcus, chasing Arya and Dev around the yard, offering to clear the table so her mom wouldn't have to. She could imagine sitting in the passenger seat, pleasantly full and sleepy, as Alex drove them home. She could imagine slipping under the sheets together, lazy smiles on their faces, a perfect end to a perfect weekend.

And then she felt the cracks in her heart grow another nanometer. Because she gave that up when she left. And she had no right to be sad when it was her own choices that had made that future impossible. She took another sip of wine.

Max nudged her back into the conversation.

"I've got to say," Marcus was saying as he twisted a beer bottle to inspect the label, "this isn't my favorite brew."

"No?" Alex asked. "Too dark for you?"

Marcus laughed. "A bit, yeah."

Bridget blinked. Alex was *teasing* him.

"Maybe stick with Life on the Berm instead, then," Alex suggested.

"Yeah, I think I will," Marcus said. He flicked a finger gun at Alex. "Still, points for trying."

"Wait. The beer's yours, too?" Bridget asked. No one had told her *anything*. Now she looked like a callous idiot for not knowing any of this stuff.

"Yeah," Alex said, "I opened up the brewery last year."

"Wow, that's... That's awesome. Congratulations."

Alex tipped her head. "Thank you."

"She's quite the entrepreneur," Evelyn said, beaming.

"What's next? A bookstore?" Jaya asked.

"Ooh, it could be a foreign-language bookstore," Marcus said.

"In a small town like this? I don't think there's really a need for it, do you? It'd be fun, though," Alex said, before taking a bite of lasagna.

"Oh, yeah," Max chimed in, "Bridget said you liked to read. A couple months ago, she gave me this book about the history of Mongolia. Said it was your favorite. I loved it!" Grinning, he switched his gaze back and forth between her and Alex. "So thanks for the indirect book recommendation."

"Yeah, I've read that," Alex said. "No problem, I guess. It's good." She shrugged. "I don't read much history anymore. No point in dwelling on the past."

Bridget gulped down half her glass of wine. Logically, of course, she knew that Alex would have changed. It'd been five years, after all. Hard for anything to stay still that long. But it was Alex, a woman she knew like her second self—except she didn't, not anymore.

It was like the Alex she'd loved and the Alex that existed now were two entirely different people. This Alex was more guarded, less quick with a smile. Some of it was because of her dad's sudden death, but how much was her own fault for leaving? She'd thought keeping up with things back home would be too hard, but no matter how hard it might've been, it would've been ten times easier than this, than thinking life would stay still while she moved on and then coming back to find how wrong that was.

"Oh, no?" Max asked, eyebrows raised as he darted a glance at Bridget. "So, what do you like to read now?"

"I've been reading a lot of sci-fi, actually. I like thinking about the future." Alex said it so casually, but Bridget caught the subtle bite in her tone.

Without thinking, she set her balled-up napkin beside her plate and got up. "I have to, um…" She didn't even finish the excuse as she left the room, feeling every pair of eyes watching her exit.

In the kitchen, she braced herself on the sink. "Oh, my God," she breathed, "I can't do this. I can't do this."

"Yes, you can," Jaya's voice said behind her. She stepped closer and rubbed a hand up and down Bridget's back. "You're so strong, Bridget."

"I'm not. I'm a coward who should've stayed and helped her through it. I should've found a way. Isn't that what people do for love? What if I made a giant mistake?"

Jaya squeezed her shoulder. "If you did, then you're owning up to it now. And you've got a big, beautiful heart that will help you make up for that mistake."

"How can she do this? How can she sit in the same room as me and not *care*?"

"I promise you she does. She's just as affected as you are."

"Yeah?" Bridget chuckled through the tears that were threatening to stream from her eyes. "Then why doesn't she act like it?"

"Oh, sweetie," said Jaya. "Because she's had so much more time to practice. Every person in this town has confronted her with this in one way or another over the years. She couldn't get away from the memory of you, not here. It's still your first week." Jaya wiped at Bridget's tears. "Don't beat yourself up, okay?"

Bridget nodded, and Jaya left her alone then to collect herself. She splashed water on her face in a half-hearted attempt to clear up the redness and, after a few more minutes, went back in.

The change of scenery as they moved into the living room was good, and Alex was relieved when the conversation thinned enough to not demand her attention. She took a seat at the edge of the red microfiber couch. She sat here almost every week, but it felt different this time. Everything felt different now, and she was out of sorts about it. Even the normally cushy couch was uncomfortable.

Maybe Alex had overestimated her own strength. Maybe she should bow out of Sunday dinners until Bridget left again.

Bridget didn't get to do this. She didn't get to disappear for years and then suddenly show up and expect everything to be the same. Alex's life might have revolved around Bridget once—it had, oh, God, it had—but not anymore. Her life was her own, and if Bridget was going to be in it, as a friend or maybe as something else someday, then Bridget had to accept that.

Friends. Friends. Alex repeated it to herself. Maybe if she said it enough times, she'd start to believe it was an actual possibility.

She came back to the conversation just in time to hear Max ask, "This is junior prom?" He pointed to a picture frame on the mantle. Even from the couch, she knew it was the one she avoided every visit. The one of her and Bridget in complementary tuxes—all because Alex hadn't felt comfortable in a dress and Bridget had wanted to make the night special. And that was before they'd dated.

Chuckling, Max said to Bridget, "You were a rebel, huh?"

"You have no idea," Evelyn said, looking pointedly at Bridget. "Maybe I should go get the photo albums."

Bridget covered her face. "Oh, my God, Mom. Please don't."

But Evelyn was already getting up and disappearing upstairs.

Alex's stomach roiled. She could accept Bridget's reappearance, accept that their spheres would overlap once again for a little while, but she didn't need to sit around and reminiscence. Reminiscing only bred resentment. "I'm sorry," she said, standing. "I just…I need some air."

Before anyone could react, she pushed out of her seat, strode through the living room, and stumbled out the door. The cool autumn air hit her face; she tilted her head back and inhaled deeply.

She should leave. The first thing she'd had to push herself to learn after the breakup was how to take care of herself, and leaving a situation that messed her up this badly was the definition of self-care.

Her respite was cut short when the door opened behind her.

"Are you all right?"

Bridget.

Alex ran her fingers through her hair to give herself time to think. "No, I don't think so. I'm sorry. Give my apologies to Evelyn."

"No."

"What?"

"You can do that yourself. If you want to leave, come inside and tell my mom yourself."

Alex balked. She stuffed her hands into her jeans pockets. She didn't even have her coat. Couldn't remember to breathe. Couldn't remember her coat. God, Bridget turned her into a loser. She turned around. "What do you want from me, Bridget?"

Bridget stood on the porch, arms curled around her stomach, though whether from the chill or something else, Alex couldn't tell. She shook her head, shrugged her shoulders. "I don't know. This just…doesn't seem sustainable, what we're doing." Much more quietly, she asked, "Do you still hate me?"

Alex opened her mouth, but nothing coherent came out. Once upon a time, she'd been very close to that. But now? No, she didn't. She was just angry and confused, and no amount of time would make that go away.

There was no hatred there. It was just...pain she didn't know where to focus, so she threw it back to the person who caused it in the first place.

Alex looked at the grass by her feet.

"What's this even accomplishing?" Bridget asked.

But she didn't sound angry. She just sounded...sad. Like Alex used to be.

When Alex didn't answer, Bridget continued, "Hanging onto your loathing like it's the only thing you've got left? I can't even get you to look at me long enough for me to apologize."

Alex looked up sharply. She hadn't even realized...

"Maybe that suits you now," Bridget said, "but what about a year from now? Five? When you look back on this moment, this week, this visit will you regret your decision not to have a real honest-to-God conversation with me?"

"An honest conversation?" Alex stepped forward, voice rising. "You were the one who left without one of those. You can't just come here and expect me to give you that courtesy when you never gave it to me."

"Alex, that's not what I... I don't expect anything of you."

"But you do," Alex said. "You want me to act like you didn't break my heart. You want everything to go back to the way it was. Well, we can't, Bridget. We can't ever go back to that."

Bridget bit her lip as she collected herself. Then she walked down the porch steps to stand right in front of Alex. "I was young, and I was scared, and I was stupid. I loved you so fucking much, but I didn't know how to help you."

Alex covered her face with her palms. She didn't want to hear this. She didn't want to hear how she wasn't good enough, how music called to Bridget and she couldn't stay stuck with a woman like Alex, how Alex could never have been good enough for someone with dreams as big as Bridget's.

"And maybe I didn't know how to help, but you didn't give me an inch," Bridget continued. "You share the blame here, too."'

That—*that* stopped Alex. That enraged Alex. Yeah, she'd needed some space to process her dad's death, but all Bridget had needed to do was wait. She couldn't even do that. "I'm not the one who gave up on us."

"But you were the one who pushed me away."

Alex reeled back. *Bridget* was the one who had left, not her. "Everything was always about you, wasn't it? I'm sorry you weren't the center of my fucking universe for a few goddamn months."

"That's…" Bridget tightened her jaw.

"What?" Alex demanded.

But Bridget only straightened and backed away. The fire in her eyes had died. "Nothing. It's nothing."

No, it was something. What was she going to accuse Alex of now? "Bridget."

But Bridget was halfway up the porch steps. "You know what? I'm obviously upsetting you, and this obviously isn't working, so just go. I'll tell my mom you got a headache."

She disappeared inside before Alex could get a word in.

Staring at the closed door, at the wreath that swung gently from the impact, Alex blew out a long sigh. It was for the best. Neither of them wanted to have this conversation anyway, and if this had showed her anything, it was that she wasn't ready to let go of her anger. Maybe she never would be.

Chapter Six

Then

ALEX RUBBED HER EYES AS she stared at the glaring laptop screen. It was past eleven PM, and she wanted nothing more than to curl up in bed with Bridget. But it turned out that getting by as fresh graduates, even on two combined incomes, wasn't as easy as some people made it out to be. She tapped the spacebar lazily. Freelance translation wasn't as exciting as she'd expected, either.

Her earbuds were pulled from her ears, arms slipped around her shoulders, and a chin came to rest on her head. Alex hummed in delight.

"Babe," Bridget whined. "It's cold in bed without you."

"There's an extra blanket in the closet. And it's summer."

"You're cruel."

Laughing, Alex latched onto Bridget's arms. "I'm also working."

"Can't you take a break?"

"If I take any more breaks, I'll never finish."

"This break is different. This break has me."

Before Alex could protest, Bridget plopped into her lap. She was wearing her Pitt sweatshirt despite the warm summer night. Alex's arms snaked around her of their own accord. She really should finish this tonight, but Bridget's grapefruit shampoo proved more enticing. She buried her nose in her girlfriend's hair.

"I think I know something that'll cheer you up," Bridget said, snagging the mouse and minimizing the current document.

"Oh, yeah?" Alex murmured. "I can think of a few things."

"Hey, I thought you said you had to finish."

"Oh, I'll finish, all right, and so will you."

Bridget jabbed her elbow gently into Alex's ribs. "You're bad."

"You love it."

"Look."

The local animal shelter's website filled the screen, displaying scrolling pictures of adoptable cats and dogs.

"Shelter animals?" Alex asked. "Their cuteness cheers me up, but the fact that they all need to be adopted does not."

"That's why we should adopt one!" Bridget's eyes were wide with excitement and hope. "Giving even just one a good home is worthwhile, isn't it?"

"Of course," Alex said through a sigh, "but I don't know. It might be hard since we don't have regular schedules."

"But between the two of us, we could work it out. He'll keep us company when the other's at work." Bridget clicked a few times and landed on a photo of a black and white pit bull. "Look at this cutie!"

"Benjamin? That's a person name, not a dog name." Still, he was adorable. All dogs were. And those big brown eyes weren't sad because he was waiting for a forever home. They were just his eyes. At least, that was what Alex told herself.

Bridget swiveled to latch her arms around Alex's neck. "We'll call him Benny. Or change his name. The shelter doesn't care as long as he has a good home."

"A dog's a lot of money. Half our diet is already ninety-seven-cent noodles."

Bridget pressed her forehead to Alex's. "Then we'll skimp on going out, and I could always ask my mom for some money. She's happy to help."

"Bridge..."

"Look." Bridget pressed a soft kiss to Alex's lips. "I know it's a lot to consider, and I don't expect an answer right now. We can talk about it again in a week, okay? And I really did think the cute pictures would help."

"They did." Mostly Bridget did, by reminding her that the sooner she finished this project, the sooner they got to snuggle.

"I'll go make you a cup of tea."

Alex pushed forward for another kiss. "Thank you."

Bridget padded into the kitchen, the sway of her hips mesmerizing in those little boxer shorts.

"Hey," Alex said, causing Bridget to turn. "I love you."

Bridget smirked. "I know."

Two days later, Benjamin—Benny—lay stretched out on a brand-new dog bed, exhausted from the arduousness of being adopted.

Alex sat nearby on the couch, her leg jiggling as she checked her phone for the twelfth time in a minute. They could make it work. She and Bridget could make anything work. Bridget didn't need to know that Alex's dad had pitched in for the adoption fee and all the necessities, at least not for a few weeks.

The key turned in the door. Bridget walked in, shuffling through the day's mail. "Babe, your dad sent a letter. He knows he can just call you, right? That's adorable, though. Tell him he can send me letters, too."

Alex dried her palms on her jeans and cleared her throat.

"Or not. That's your thing. I get it," Bridget said, still not looking up as she walked into the kitchen. "The rest are just bills. Blah."

Alex stood. "Bridge."

Bridget threw the mail onto the kitchen table and turned to open the fridge. "Yeah?"

"After you showed me Benny's picture the other day, I just couldn't seem to get him out of my head."

Bridget paused, shut the fridge, and edged out of the kitchen. When her gaze landed on the sleeping dog, her face lit up. "You didn't!"

Alex shuffled her weight. A blush rose to her cheeks. She lived for making Bridget happy.

"Benny!" Bridget shouted, alerting the dog. She kneeled down, and Benny lumbered to his feet to sniff the new arrival. He licked her hand. "I think he likes me," she said, nearing a squeal.

"I think he does," Alex said.

Bridget scratched the dog's ears. "I will pet you later, in two seconds, but first..." She stood and threw her arms around Alex. "I think you *love* me."

Alex pulled away, grinning. "I still do, but you've been edged out of the number-one spot."

"For Benny?"

"For Benny."

Bridget shrugged. "I'm weirdly okay with that."

Alex laughed, and when Bridget kissed her, all her worries slipped away. All that mattered was here in this tiny living room.

Now

"You're a mess, you know that?" Lu said, laughing, once Alex finished recounting the dinner debacle from a few days back.

Lu, Jordan, and Owen were lined up on stools at the bar. At least Owen, with little Keiko strapped to his chest, had the decency to look embarrassed for her.

Alex rolled her eyes as she refilled Lu's beer. "Yes, I'm well aware. You can stop laughing now."

"No, I really can't," Lu said between laughs. "Too funny."

Jordan smacked her on the back of the head, and she finally shut up. "Give her a break. She's obviously having a crisis."

Alex held up her hands. "Oh, my God. I'm not having a crisis. I'm just..." In fact, she was still simmering with anger. She picked up a clean rag and started wiping out glasses to give her hands something to do. "Every time I go to the grocery store or the post office—hell, when I serve a customer here, everyone has this look in their eye. They all want to give me advice on my love life. Do you know how invasive that is, to have a whole town know your baggage? I just need some breathing room."

"Are you sure you're not imagining it?" Owen asked.

"I'm sure."

"Then maybe they're onto something. When you look at her, when she walks into the bar, how do you feel?"

Alex crossed her arms on the bar top and slumped down. She felt a lot of things, and most of the time, she couldn't make sense of any of them. But the overriding emotion was always anger. Anger mixed with pain.

"She looks pretty good. Does that...stir anything in you?" Lu asked.

Alex threw the rag at her.

"Hey! I'm just trying to help!"

"You're not," Jordan said, smirking. "You're causing trouble."

Lu waggled her shoulder. "What can I say? It's what I do best!"

Alex rolled her eyes at her friends, but fondly.

"Maybe you need some time to yourselves, away from everybody and everything. Away from potential interruptions, too," said Owen.

"As far as I'm concerned," Alex said, "nothing will come out of that conversation anyway, so why try?"

"Just ask her to meet you in a private place so you can talk without all this." He gestured around, meaning the entire town.

"He's right. You have shit to talk out," Jordan said.

"You're only agreeing because you're married to him."

"I picked a smart one." Jordan wrapped a hand around Owen's neck, pulled him in to kiss his cheek, and then bent to plop a kiss on Keiko's head.

"One problem," Alex said. "I'm not interested."

"Well," Lu started.

She straightened up, and Alex knew that posture. She was about to be a little shit.

"It doesn't matter if you're not interested. You may think you're over it, but this fucked you both up for a long time. The only way you move forward is if you two talk."

Alex tightened her jaw and shook her head. "I wasn't the one who left."

"Did you give her much reason to stay?" Lu asked.

"Hey," Jordan said. "It's not about blame. It's about not walling yourself off for the rest of your life."

All three of her friends looked at Alex expectantly. She leaned on the bar and lowered her head onto her arms. It wasn't that she was broken. It was just that she wasn't all that interested in a relationship. Not right now, at least. Probably not for a while. And that preference had nothing to do with the fact that Bridget had left her. She wasn't some gaping wound that needed to be stitched up. She could take care of herself. She *was* taking care of herself.

She let out a frustrated growl.

The jingling of the bell above the door was so commonplace that she didn't even notice Riley coming back from her break until she walked behind the bar.

"I'm back," Riley said. "I can take over, Boss."

Alex stowed the rag beneath the bar. "Thanks. I have to go catch up on some paperwork. Holler if you need me."

She bid her friends a good-bye that was only slightly frosty and headed to her office, where she lost herself in work until a knock sounded on the frame of her open door.

"Come in," Alex said without looking up.

"Hey," Bridget said. She took a hesitant step inside.

"Oh, um…" Alex stood up quickly, swiping a hand through her hair. Was there a single place Bridget couldn't haunt her? "I didn't expect you. Sorry. Did we have an appointment?"

God, she was such an idiot. She winced at her own rambling. Why would Bridget have set up an appointment? And on a weeknight? She took a deep breath.

Bridget smiled gently. "No, no appointment. I just came by to bring you this." She held out Alex's coat. "And to apologize."

Alex took the coat and hung it on her chair. She rounded her desk to lean against it and cross her arms. "Apologize?"

"Yeah," Bridget said, twiddling her fingers. "For pushing you to be friends. Clearly, I hurt you even worse than I thought, so I came to apologize for that. And to tell you I won't bother you anymore. Max and I won't come to the bar anymore. We probably won't even hang around town." Her smile turned sad. "It'll be like we're not even here."

"That's…" Alex trailed off because her mouth was way too dry. She licked her lips and fought to swallow.

Bridget turned, a question in her eyes, like she wondered if Alex would object.

Distance was exactly what Alex needed. All she wanted to do was keep living her life without interruption. Bridget threatened that. And yet… Alex didn't own the whole town. She could find refuge in her own house. She could limit the amount of times she'd be likely to run into Bridget. She could handle this.

Alex cleared her throat. "That's not necessary. I mean, it's your town, too. I don't want to keep you from it, especially since…"

"Since I haven't visited in years." Bridget chest rose with relief, but her brow furrowed. "I thought that was what you wanted, though. After dinner…"

God, they were always talking in half-sentences, never sure whether to finish their thoughts, always dreading how the other would react.

Owen was right. They needed breathing space, time alone, someplace without the pressure of the town closing in on them.

And now here they were, and they couldn't find anything to say to one another. Not anything real, at least.

The problem, she thought, was that she'd never really expected Bridget to come back. They ran in totally separate spheres now. For half a decade, it seemed Bridget had pulled up her roots entirely, which meant Alex had never thought through what she wanted to say because she never thought she'd get the chance.

And the problem with not thinking about what she wanted to say meant she never really thought about how she *felt*, either, beyond the surface-level anger that had carried her through five whole years. Now, she couldn't force any of that emotion into comprehensible words.

She breathed in deeply. When she finally looked up, Bridget's expression was unreadable, and her eyes were dark.

Half a second later, before Alex could process anything, Bridget surged forward, took Alex's face between her hands, and kissed her. She wrapped her arms around Alex's waist, and Alex's mouth opened immediately beneath hers. Like instinct. Like muscle memory. Like: *This, this person is mine and so are those lips and so is everything she is.*

She tasted like beer and peppermint. She tasted like memories.

Familiar. That was what this felt like. Five years, eighteen hundred days, and she hadn't forgotten the shape of Bridget's lips or the press of their bodies or the way Bridget's breath hitched when Alex ran her thumb over her hip. Bridget was etched into her, a tattoo she could never be rid of, its ink poisoning her blood.

Bridget snaked a hand beneath Alex's T-shirt. Alex shivered.

If this was what it meant to die a slow and agonizing death, Alex accepted the poison willingly because, with the two of them, pain and pleasure went hand-in-hand. At least they'd stopped pretending they didn't.

Bridget walked them backward, straight into the desk. Alex felt the reverberation through her body as the backs of her thighs hit the wood, and Bridget took the momentary pause to change the angle of the kiss, brushing her nose over Alex's. The move, oddly tender, sent another shiver down Alex's spine.

Alex moaned. Her nerves were on fire. Her whole body was on fire. Bridget's hands were on her hips, on her stomach, brushing her breasts over her bra.

Alex bit down on Bridget's lower lip, eliciting a growl that, in turn, elicited a pang of desire in Alex's stomach. She whined when Bridget pulled away. Ten minutes ago, she would've been ashamed of herself for wanting her ex so vocally. But ten minutes ago, Bridget wasn't kissing her like they were twenty-three years old again. This kind of visceral attraction was hard to fight.

Smirking, Bridget pushed Alex's papers off the desktop and lifted her onto it. Her panties were probably soaked, but with Bridget's fingers curling tightly on her hips, Alex couldn't bring herself to care.

"Fuck," she gasped. She latched her legs around Bridget's waist, tugging her even closer, and kissed her again, stopping Bridget's smug laughter.

Memories flashed through Alex's mind. The kitchen in their tiny apartment in the city. The roof under the stars. The private study room in the university library. This was one of the many ways Bridget had loved Alex, unraveling and needy and affectionate.

Had loved? Or was it *still loved*? Was this more for Bridget than it was for Alex? Was it more than the specific combination of proximity and a need for release? Because that was all it was for Alex. A purely physical thing. Wasn't it?

She broke off the kiss, breathing hard. "Stop," she said. "Stop. This isn't... We shouldn't..."

"Why not?" Bridget murmured. She cupped Alex's cheek to pull their foreheads together. "Have you found anything with anyone that feels as right as we do together?"

Alex licked her lips, bruised by the pressure of Bridget's. She didn't have a good answer, but not because it didn't exist. Only because her head spun and she couldn't think straight. Physically, they'd always been a fantastic match. But they weren't eighteen anymore. They couldn't skate by on physical attraction.

"Alex..." Bridget breathed against her lips. She brushed Alex's hair behind her ears. "Oh, my beautiful, darling Alex, tell me—"

"Hey, Boss. Oh!"

Bridget jumped away from Alex as Riley stood, shocked, just inside the door.

"Um, I thought my question was important, but I see now that it isn't, so..." Riley scurried back into the hallway and closed the door behind her.

Alex blew out a quick breath. She could still feel Bridget pressed against her, her hands gripping Alex's hips. She could still taste her, taste the tang of hops on her tongue.

"I should..." Bridget said, backing away.

When Alex looked up, Bridget looked down.

"Yeah," Alex said, nodding like a damned bobble head. "Yeah." She didn't even know what she was agreeing to. What was even happening? What had they just done?

"So..."

"Right."

Then Bridget was backing into the door, fumbling it open, and walking through. But she stopped in the doorway to glance at Alex, her expression heavy with desire and....regret?

Chest heaving with a well of emotions that Bridget's kiss had incited, emotions she hadn't given thought to in much too long, Alex watched Bridget walk away. Again.

And when she was gone, Alex raised a hand to her still-tingling lips.

Softly, in the safety of her dingy office, she whispered, "Fuck."

Bridget stumbled out of the bar without paying any attention to where she was walking or who she was walking into, her mind consumed with Alex.

Alex's hands in her hair.

Alex's legs around her waist.

Alex's lips against hers.

The cold air stung, but it was nothing compared to the shock she had gotten in that office.

She slowed her steps. Once she buttoned her coat, it was a pleasant enough night, and she didn't want to waste it.

As she strolled down Main Street, she let the memories that had been bumping up against the barrier of her mental reservoir through. The moment she let go, the moment she let that wall collapse, she felt freer, lighter than she had in ages.

There was the park where they'd sneak out to swing beneath the stars. There was the diner where they'd hang out on Friday nights because they had nothing better to do. There was the library, where they'd spend afternoons sprawled on the bean bags in the reading room as sunlight poured in.

So much of her life here revolved around Alex, and when she'd cut off Alex, she'd cut off the rest of it, too. She'd cut off Edna from the diner who occasionally gave them pie on the house. She'd cut off George at the library, who was always ready with a new book recommendation. She wanted them back. She wanted this whole town back. But most, most, most of all, she wanted Alex back.

She laughed, ran her hands through her hair. *Alex had kissed her back.* She was giddy with the taste of Alex on her lips. Because that was not the kiss of a disinterested ex-girlfriend. That was the kiss of a woman who'd finally let herself *want* without any thought of the consequences, and Bridget knew because that's exactly how she'd felt, too.

A brief, blissful moment interrupted too quickly. Bridget could curse Riley for her bad timing.

She stopped walking.

Riley hadn't interrupted them.

Alex had.

Alex had wanted to stop.

Oh, God. Had Alex regretted the kiss as soon as it'd happened?

Horrified, Bridget covered her mouth with her hands.

Shit.

A door right in front of her opened with a jingle. She stepped out of the way and pressed her back against the brick wall. She felt stupid. She felt *sick.*

Alex held so much anger now. Bridget remembered a soft, sweet woman, someone who'd had trouble opening up but had never been actively hurtful. Bridget only half-recognized this Alex. The change couldn't be completely contributed to her, could it? Even if it couldn't, how were they supposed to fix this? They couldn't even sit down and have a civil conversation.

Across the street, the town grocery store's lights were on. Not bothering to use the crosswalk, she jogged over and into the store.

As she headed for the frozen section, a dry laugh escaped her throat when she passed the beer display.

Life on the Berm. Fitting. When she got to the register, the clerk gave her a sympathetic look, though Bridget couldn't tell if it was because all she was buying was a carton of ice cream and a plastic spoon or because she was Bridget Callahan and all she was buying was a carton of ice cream and a plastic spoon.

With her purchase in a plastic bag, she exited the grocery store and headed toward the one place in town no one would look for her, the one place she could be alone with no pressure from anyone—intended or otherwise—over how to act.

The theater was just a few blocks over, down a side street without much traffic.

The theater where they had their first kiss. Also fitting.

The hardware store and the music shop across the street were closed for the night, and no foot traffic meant she didn't have a problem sneaking in. The padlock on the far right door was broken but still on the chain. In a decade, no one had bothered to replace it, and once she got inside and shined her phone flashlight around, it was clear the secret had stayed well kept. Kids these days must be less curious. Or maybe they just had more activities and less free time to go running around town on the hunt for secret hiding places.

Bridget sighed as she moved through the lobby. Despite the cobwebs that lived in the corners of the walls and ceiling, there was a somber elegance to this place. The red velvet carpet. The naked bulbs around the ticket booth window. Remnants of an earlier, fancier time.

When she opened the door to the theater floor, her hand came away covered in dust. She wiped it on her jeans. Dust covered the entire theater, too, and a good number of the seats were broken. She walked down the left aisle and up the stage stairs to sit on the top step.

It was dark in here, but it wasn't scary. With all the wonderful memories it housed, it couldn't be.

She took out her phone, turned on Do Not Disturb mode, and switched off the screen. She set the phone on the stage face-up so the flashlight illuminated a small circle next to her. Then she opened the ice cream and scooped out a mammoth spoonful.

Well, damn. She'd really fucked everything up, and she had no clue how to make it right.

Most nights, Alex loved the bar. She loved the camaraderie, and she loved that everyone who stepped through the door shared in it. She loved the familiar faces, familiar smiles, familiar laughter. Tonight, though, it was all too loud. She didn't have to hear the thoughts circling through her head to know who they were about.

When it came time for her break, she shrugged into her jacket and headed outside. Her bad days usually meant she had too much energy and nowhere to put it. Those were the days she went on ten- or twelve-mile runs, did an hour with the heavy bag, exercised until exhaustion turned her body to jelly and made her mind go blank.

She wasn't used to this new type of restlessness that thrummed through her and kept her unsteady, so she couldn't treat it with the same old medicine. Instead of pushing herself to the brink and collapsing for an extra-long night of dreamless sleep, she focused on the cool air moving in and out of her lungs. She focused on the sidewalk beneath her feet and on putting one foot in front of the other. She focused on calming the tempest that raged in her mind.

Bridget had *kissed* her, and Alex had been reeling ever since. She thought at the most, Bridget wanted to clear the air, wanted forgiveness for the way she'd left.

But to be kissed—like *that*—had only dragged Alex back in time. She ran her fingers over her lips, still feeling the press of Bridget's.

Abruptly, she pulled her hand away. So it was a really good kiss. That wasn't enough to suck her back under. If she really needed to be kissed, she could go to that lesbian bar in the city and find someone who'd take her home and keep her warm for a night.

She was headed nowhere in particular, hardly paying attention to her meandering path until a car honked at her. She waved an apology, jogged across the rest of the street, and hopped onto the sidewalk.

Directly in front of the theater.

If she was looking for a sign that she needed to face her demons, no sense in looking any further.

The lock was still busted. She had been meaning to change it for years, just to keep the space that was so precious to them private, but she'd never gotten around to it. She'd let her life get too busy as a way to distract herself from all the memories, all the hurt.

It was funny that the memories didn't seem so painful right now. The pain was still present, but mingled with…sweetness.

Edging into the darkened lobby, she turned on the flashlight on her phone.

She walked into the main theater and stopped just inside the doors. On the stage was a diluted light pointing at the ceiling. A phone flashlight. At the sound of the doors closing, a figure sat up.

A pit settled in Alex's stomach. It could only be one person, the only person she wasn't sure she could talk to, the only person she *needed* to talk to.

The beam of light moved, and Bridget called, "Hello? Who's there?"

Alex cleared her throat.

Bridget was already up and walking down the aisle toward her. She held the light above her head. "Alex?" she asked as she approached.

"I didn't… I didn't know you were here," Alex said, but the words *I'll go* got stuck on the way out.

"Oh." Bridget's gaze dropped. "So…my mom didn't ask you to look for me?"

"Why would she?"

Bridget shrugged, clearly embarrassed. "I needed some time to think."

Alex nodded, understanding despite the words left unsaid. She shoved her hands into her pockets. For the first time since Bridget had returned, she didn't feel completely unbalanced. Only mostly.

Before she could think up a way to extract herself from the situation, Bridget said, "Talk with me?"

Alex licked her lips. Last time they'd tried that, it hadn't turned out so well. This was different, though, wasn't it? They weren't so conscious of Bridget's family right inside the house, and somehow, here in this theater, the past wasn't so much a monstrous specter than it was an old, neglected friend.

"Five minutes," Bridget said, voice cracking. "All I'm asking for is five minutes."

She could do five minutes. With a nod, Alex followed her to the stage, where they sat on the steps, the light between them. Alex sniffed and rested her arms on her knees. They had to clear the air eventually. Maybe the sooner they did that, the sooner Bridget could go back to her real life. That would be better for both of them.

Wouldn't it?

"Do you remember the first time we kissed?" Bridget asked.

Something squeezed Alex's heart. "Of course I do." How could she forget one of the defining moments of her life?

"This feels a lot like that."

"That's just because we're in the same place." It wasn't anything more than that.

"It means something, though, doesn't it? That we both showed up here tonight?"

Alex rubbed her eyes. "No, Bridget, it doesn't mean anything. It's just a coincidence." They were two of a handful of people who even knew the theater could still be accessed.

Bridget's sigh was too loud in the empty theater. "Why do you do this?"

"Do what?"

Bridget gestured erratically. "Act like I meant nothing to you. Act like we don't have years of history."

Because you broke my heart, Alex wanted to say, but she bit her lip instead. Then she asked, "Why'd you kiss me?"

Bridget was quiet a long time, her unfocused gaze on the aisle floor. This was what they did now, weighed their words until they found some that wouldn't destroy what little footing they'd gained.

"I wanted to," she finally said. "But I shouldn't have because you didn't want it. I'm sorry."

Had Alex wanted it? Because despite all her anger, despite the bitterness eating up her insides, she'd kissed Bridget back. For a moment, just a moment, her knees had gone weak and she'd wanted to turn back the clock to simpler times. She was stronger now, yeah, but less happy.

"Do you have any feelings for me at all besides anger?" Bridget murmured.

Now that thing squeezed Alex's heart so hard it stopped altogether.

"I act like this—angry—because…" Her shoulders heaved. It felt like she couldn't quite get enough breath in her lungs. "You made me feel…" She searched for a single word into which to distill the most devastating event of her life. "Worthless," she breathed, and with the word came all the sadness she'd kept bottled up.

"Oh, Lex," Bridget breathed.

Tears pricked at Alex's eyes, and she had to swallow the lump in her throat. She'd spent so long convincing herself otherwise that it was almost cathartic to speak the truth into the world. "Like I was too broken to deserve to be loved."

Bridget lifted her head to look straight into Alex's eyes. Even in the dim light, Bridget's eyes were cornflower-field blue, and Alex had never failed to imagine a future just as sunny every time she looked into them.

"You told me you loved me and that you'd take care of me, and as soon as things got difficult, you left." Alex shook her head. "That's not what people do to people they love."

Bridget started to reach for Alex's hands but stopped herself. "I didn't do it because I didn't love you. And I would trade every drop of my success to not have made that decision," she said firmly.

The thing around Alex's heart gave one last hard squeeze that sent fractures throughout. Her voice cracked along with it. "It doesn't matter now, does it?"

Didn't someone say you couldn't go home again? You could never go back to an old love. You were a different person. They were a different person. It was impossible.

The sooner Alex came to terms with that, the sooner Bridget's presence would stop messing with her head.

"I should go," she said, getting to her feet. She wiped away the tears burning at her eyes, brushed off the seat of her pants, and, sniffling, took a moment to gather herself. "Are you okay to get home?"

Bridget held an empty ice-cream pint in the light. "Been hitting the hard stuff."

Despite the tightness in her chest and throat, Alex chuckled. "Drive safe."

"You, too."

Alex bit her lip as she trudged down the stairs and up the aisle.

"And, Alex?"

Alex slowed her stride but didn't pause.

"Thank you for your honesty."

Bridget returned to a quiet house. Max was asleep, but her mom was still awake, reading a book on the living room couch. Cozy. Bridget joined her, tucking her legs under her and pulling a blanket onto her lap.

Evelyn took one look at her face, patted her knee, and said, "I'll go make you a cup of tea." She slid a bookmark into the hardback mystery and slipped out of the room.

Bridget toyed with the edge of the blanket. The entire walk home, her mind had been numb, but she couldn't run from this any longer.

Her mom returned minutes later with a steaming cup of tea that warmed Bridget's palms. She wished that warmth would spread to the inside, too. Evelyn picked up her book again. She didn't press because she knew she didn't have to. For a few minutes, Bridget simply blew on her tea and watched her turn pages.

Once the tea had cooled enough to take a few tiny sips, she said, "I went to the theater."

"Oh? How is it inside?"

"Pretty much the same. Dustier, I guess."

"It's a shame no one's done anything with it. A lovely building but a little impractical."

Bridget frowned. That theater could be useful in a lot of ways. The high school could perform there. Community theater groups. The town could host its annual Christmas party there. Hell, she could buy it and use it to practice. The acoustics were incredible.

"I saw Alex," Bridget said, staring into her tea. "Just for a few minutes. We finally talked. A little bit."

Evelyn finally took her gaze from her book, but again, she didn't say anything.

"I should have listened to you. I should have given her more time," Bridget said.

"Sometimes," Evelyn said gently, "what makes a relationship not work isn't the people. It's timing. You were ready to spread your wings and take more from life, she needed a bit more time, and there's no easy answer there. You can't keep blaming yourself after all this time."

"I can, actually, because it's my fault." Bridget's voice shook, and she swallowed to steady it. "I promised her I loved her, and then just when she was hurting the most, I broke that promise."

"Love doesn't always mean forever, sweetheart, and you can't always protect the people you love. If you hadn't left, you still might've broken up down the road. Alex still would've been hurt. *You* still would've been hurt."

Though the tea had cooled somewhat, it scalded Bridget's throat. "There's no point in talking about what-ifs, though, is there? All that matters is what happened, and what happened was because of a decision I made. I thought it would snap her out of her grief and shock her back into the land of the living. I thought she was strong enough that I could force her. But I destroyed her, Mom." How did she make amends for that? Bridget set down her tea so she could wipe her eyes on the edge of the blanket. "She's like a different person. And I did that, Mom. I did that to her."

Frowning, Evelyn put a hand over Bridget's. "You also haven't spoken in five years. Five years changes a person. We're only living if we're growing. Who knows how Alex would have turned out if you had stayed? Like you said, no point in dwelling on what-ifs."

The only problem was, Bridget's mind wouldn't let them go. Well, it wouldn't let *one* go. What if she had stayed? What if she had been patient and loving and compassionate enough to stay and work through Alex's pain?

Evelyn reached over to wipe the tears from Bridget's cheeks. "Alex is sometimes angry now, yes. And sometimes she's happy. All the things inside her heart now are the things that were there when you fell in love with her. Imagine if you take a bottle and fill it with layers of different colored sand. When you shake it up, it doesn't look the same, but all the same sand is still there. If you hadn't shaken the bottle, someone or something else would have, and you have to accept that. And if you want to have Alex in your life, you have to accept her for who she is *now*, not who she was when you were eighteen."

Bridget sniffled and wiped her eyes on her sleeve. "What if Alex doesn't want *me* in *her* life?"

"Then you have to accept her decision, sweetheart." Evelyn pressed a kiss to Bridget's temple. "Maybe right now, it doesn't seem like she wants you in her life, but, like before, maybe Alex just needs a little more time than you did to come to the realization that she does."

Chapter Seven

Then

THE APARTMENT WAS QUIET WHEN Alex walked through the front door. She was grateful it was Friday night; the mind-numbing office work was taking its toll on her, sapping her creativity. All she wanted to do was order pizza and watch crappy movies on the couch with Bridget. But the silence was so complete she wondered if Bridget was even here. Benny didn't run out to greet her either.

"Hello?" she called.

The first place she checked was the bedroom, which was dark save for the pinky-orange glow of the late-evening sun. It was enough to illuminate Bridget, asleep on the bed, Benny beside her.

Alex, careful not to wake them, quietly shuffled out of her shoes and changed into plaid sleep pants and a loose T-shirt. She padded into the kitchen to pour a glass of water and came back to set it beside the bed.

Gingerly, she sat on the edge of the mattress. "Babe," she said softly, kissing Bridget on the forehead. "I brought you some water."

Bridget stirred awake. Immediately, she curled into Alex.

"What's the matter?" Alex asked, still in that soothing voice. "Are you feeling okay?"

Bridget shook her head. "Mm-mm."

"What's wrong?"

"Headache."

Alex frowned. Bridget often got headaches, which slowed her down, and when she slowed down, she tended to get low. Not quite depressed, but Alex worried she could get there someday. "Can you sit up for me? I brought you some water. It'll help."

Bridget let Alex help her shift into a sitting position, then drank the whole glass.

Alex tucked Bridget's hair behind her ear. "Let me run you a bath."

At Bridget's nod, Alex headed into the bathroom to fill the tub. When it was over half full and the water was decently hot without being scalding, she turned off the tap and called Bridget, setting out a fresh towel while Bridget undressed and slipped into the water.

"Is there anything else I can do for you?" Alex asked, kneeling beside the tub. "I was thinking about ordering out tonight. Do you want something in particular?" Takeout was a splurge, but she was too tired to cook a proper meal.

Bridget reached out. "Stay with me? We can order dinner later."

"Okay." Alex took off her clothes and folded them into a pile.

Bridget leaned forward so Alex could climb in behind her. Once Alex was settled, she wrapped one arm around Bridget's waist as Bridget leaned back into her. With the other, she stroked Bridget's hair.

"Do you want to talk about it?" she asked.

"Not really."

Alex hummed. If Bridget wanted to talk, she'd do so in her own time. Alex busied herself instead with kneading her knuckles into Bridget's tense shoulders, working slowly and steadily, drawing out low, satisfied moans.

She grabbed a bar of soap and lathered up Bridget's shoulders, torso, and arms, then cupped warm water in her hands to rinse it off. She squeezed out a dollop of shampoo and soaped up Bridget's golden hair. When she was done rinsing it, careful not to get any suds in Bridget's eyes, Bridget leaned back once more.

The water was cooling, but Alex would stay here as long as Bridget wanted. She kept her arms wrapped around Bridget's waist, thumb moving up and down against Bridget's belly.

"Waitressing exhausts me," Bridget said eventually.

Alex pressed a light kiss to her neck. "I know, babe."

"I'm twenty-two. I shouldn't feel this tired."

No, she shouldn't. "They never should've asked you to come in to open when you closed last night." But that wasn't the root of the problem. It was just a symptom of a much bigger one, one where they were saddled with insurmountable student loan debt in a lousy economy that refused to pay a living wage.

Bridget made a small sound that Alex couldn't decipher. Then she said, "I want to be more than this. For myself. For you."

Alex hummed. Softly, she said, "Your job doesn't define you. No one's does. And we're just a few months out of school. Things will get better."

"How do you know? You know, what if this is it? What if we're stuck working multiple jobs and not having enough time for each other or the things we actually want to do with our lives?"

Alex pressed her lips to Bridget's shoulder. She knew Bridget was talking about music, her biggest love. Since they'd graduated and Bridget had taken on two different jobs, she barely had time to write or practice.

"Hey," Alex said, "just give it time. We'll figure it out, and if I have to work twelve jobs so you can quit yours and follow your dreams, I'll do it."

Bridget chuckled. "Shut up. This isn't about my dreams versus yours. It's about us, too."

"I know, babe. I know." Alex held Bridget firmly around the waist, trying to make her feel safe and secure. "One day soon, one of us will get a break, and things will fall into place. In the meantime, we've got each other, and there's no one I'd rather be struggling to build a life beside than you."

Now

Bridget woke up with a headache. She didn't want to open her eyes, but the sunlight streaming through the window had already pierced her closed lids. She'd have to get up eventually, have to face another Alex-less day. Might as well get it over with, so she dragged herself to the bathroom, where she washed her face and brushed her teeth and gulped down an entire glass of water.

She didn't even bother to put on real clothes or brush her hair or make herself presentable at all before trudging down the steps and making her way into the kitchen, where Max was banging around pots and pans.

"What the hell are you doing?" she asked.

Max paused where he was bending into a lower cabinet to give her a sheepish look. "Your mom left, and I'm having a heck of a time finding a pan."

Bridget groaned, but retrieved one of those special no-stick pans from the drawer of the island and handed it to him before collapsing into a chair.

He poured her a coffee and slid it toward her. "Drink up."

She downed half of the deliciously strong brew and leaned her cheek on the table with a sigh.

"You got back late last night," he said, his tone curious, cautious.

Closing her eyes didn't keep the memories from tormenting her—kissing Alex in her office and being interrupted, fleeing the scene and then Alex not bothering to come after her, buying a pint of chocolate chip and taking it to the theater.

She knew she hadn't done the right thing all those years ago. She knew that. But she'd thought, just maybe, that Alex was softening toward her, that Alex was realizing all the mistakes they both had made, that Alex was looking past the hurt to see that Bridget still loved her.

Bridget still loved her so fucking much. She'd known it for years, but the realization coupled with the hurt from last night and the crushing headache today brought tears to her eyes.

"Where'd you go?" Max asked gently.

"The theater. I was just…thinking about things."

"Anything I can help with?"

She smiled at his earnestness. "Not exactly, but thanks."

"Well, you'll feel better if you get some food in you. And after that, music. It'll heal your soul."

He plopped a plate in front of her. On it was a stack of three overdone pancakes.

Again, Bridget fought the urge to cry. Alex had always made the best pancakes.

Alex paused for breath. The autumn air was pleasantly cool, especially in the forest, on the mountain; it was just what she needed. She glanced behind her at Lu, still down the path a ways.

When Lu caught up, she put her hands on her hips and said, "You're not supposed to be hiking alone."

"I appreciate your concern, but I'm a grown-ass woman. I can hike alone if I want to. Besides, you're here."

"Right now, but I have a job to get back to."

"Your lunch break's not over."

"It'll be over long before we make it to the top. Look, I promised I'd meet you on my break because I knew if I didn't, you'd go anyway."

"You think I need looking after?"

Lu frowned. "I think—we all think—that Bridget coming back to town has…unnerved you. Hell, it's unnerved us all. Are we friends with her? Are we not friends?"

"I already said it was fine if you guys want to be friends with her."

"Yeah, I know. Can we please just sit and eat here?"

"Fine." But only because Lu didn't ask her to promise she wouldn't go on alone afterwards. Alex sat on the forest floor, her back against a tree.

Lu chose a fallen trunk, slung off her pack, and pulled out a sandwich and a bottle of water. Soon enough, the snow would come, and hiking would have to wait until spring. Alex wasn't looking forward to being cooped up all winter with nothing much through which to expel her energy. Maybe she'd take up skiing.

"I talked to Bridget last night," Alex said, finally getting it off her chest. If someone other than she knew, that meant the conversation, however brief, had been real.

The words hung in the air, and she could practically see the gears turning in Lu's head.

"No kidding?" Lu said.

"That's not all," Alex said. "She came to see me at the bar, to give me my coat back, and we… We kissed."

Lu's eyes went wide, but she reined in her tone. "Who kissed who?"

"She kissed me."

"So…did you kiss back?"

"Sort of." It had been instinct, muscle memory. That was all. So why did she feel so guilty about it?

"Oh."

"Oh?"

Lu swigged from her water bottle. "So, this is why you insisted on hiking today. Your awkward ass has all this anxiety to work off because you can't handle how you feel."

"I don't feel any way except angry."

"So you've said—and showed. I don't think that's true, though."

"I don't—"

"Okay, so you're not *in love* with her," Lu said, holding up a hand to shut Alex up. "But you've obviously got leftover feelings of some kind. You can't just let that shit fester. You gotta deal with it one way or another."

Alex closed her eyes, dropped her head into her hands, and breathed deeply. The cool air helped clear her head. She'd been pushing all her feelings so deep down that she'd thought they'd stay buried forever. They hadn't, though. Instead, she was dealing with a whole big mess of emotions she couldn't make sense of.

Except she wasn't dealing with it at all, was she?

When she looked up, Lu had a knowing expression on her face. Not pitying, though, which Alex appreciated.

"Being angry all the time is…exhausting."

"You could try being not angry?"

"It's not that simple, Lu."

"Why not?"

Alex took a drag from her water bottle. Out of all her friends, Lu was the one who would read into what she said next the least. Without taking her gaze from the fallen leaves scattered on the path, she said, "Because feeling anything else scares me too much."

It took most of the day for Bridget to feel like her head wasn't going to explode at the slightest noise, and she spent it lying on the couch. Max lazed at the other end as they watched cartoons with the volume low. When she felt more like normal, she ventured into the kitchen for a glass of water and some soup.

As always, the feeling that she should be writing songs nagged at her. But this was kind of a vacation; she didn't have to be writing every minute of every day. She was allowed to take a day off, allowed to let herself relax, and rest would help rejuvenate her creative juices.

She'd always had trouble with that, though.

She brought soup for Max, too, and they made it until the first commercial break before he said, "You're freaking out that we haven't gotten anything done today, aren't you?"

She frowned. "I'm not freaking out. I'm just..." The truth was that she *needed* to keep busy. She needed to keep her mind on something that wasn't Alex because if she didn't, her thoughts would take her somewhere she didn't want to go. Not at all.

Like that kiss last night. That brief, shining moment was the first time she'd felt alive, truly alive, since they'd broken up. How pathetic was that? She'd tried. She really had. Along with success as a musician, she'd found something approaching contentment. But there was no hiding from the fact that Alex still had power over her—power to make her happy, or sad

She sipped the soup, which had cooled just enough not to burn her mouth.

"I like to keep busy," was all she said.

Max snorted. "It's okay to take a day off, you know."

She hadn't had one of those in five years. When she wasn't touring or performing or shooting music videos or attending award shows, she was writing or practicing. At least a handful of hours each day. Sitting around didn't suit her.

Even if she tried, though, she wasn't in the headspace to get any writing done. Some days were like that. You couldn't force it. So they settled in for a movie marathon.

Around six, halfway into the third movie, her mom came into the living room, coat and hat on. "All right, kids, you're on your own for dinner."

Bridget sat up. "Where are you going?"

"To the town hall meeting."

Oh. Right. Her mom had an interest in those things. "What's this one about?"

Evelyn sighed. "The fall festival. And the school."

"What's up with the school?"

"Yeah, didn't it just get the money for a new roof?" Max asked with a smirk in Bridget's direction that she decidedly ignored.

"Well, yes, and that was a generous donation, but in the grand scheme of things, a roof doesn't take all that much money. The teachers' contract is up soon, and there's talk of a strike if their demands aren't met."

"That sucks," Bridget said.

Unexpectedly, Evelyn brightened. "Is that interest I hear? Does that mean you want to come?"

"Ugh, Mom. No."

But Max prodded her thigh with his bare foot. "Come on, Bridge. It'll get us out of the house, maybe make you feel like you're being productive."

Bridget gestured toward her day-old clothing. "I look like a mess. And I smell. I think."

"Well, hurry up and take a shower!" Evelyn said, clapping her hands. "Go jump in. I'm headed to the fire hall now to help set up, but you can meet me there. There will be cookies!"

Bridget rolled her eyes. Getting clean and out of the house would be good for her. So she nodded. "Fine. We'll see you there."

Alex filled a stein with beer and slid it over to a customer.

Lu, Jordan, and Owen, with little Keiko strapped to his chest, approached the bar.

"You coming to the town hall meeting?" asked Jordan.

On any other night, sure. As a local business owner, she tried to keep up with what was happening around town, tried to be a good citizen even if she was mostly disinterested. Tonight, though, her head was reeling with the ghost of Bridget's lips on hers and that thing inside her chest that had gone from an ember to an inferno in the space of a few days.

"Not tonight," she said.

"But you always come, and there will be cookies," Owen said.

"I'm just kind of wiped. Take notes for me."

"Fine, but don't expect us to bring you any cookies."

She chuckled through her nose. "Of course not."

An hour later, once the town hall was well under way and the dinner rush had died down, she let Riley know she was taking her dinner break, exchanged her apron for her jacket, and headed home. An hour wasn't much time to run home, fit in a workout, hop in the shower, and get back to the bar, but she was buzzing with excess energy, and it needed to go somewhere.

Once she was in the door, she quickly dressed in basketball shorts and a tank top. Setting her phone in the speaker cradle, she blasted upbeat music, then wrapped her hands, put on her gloves, and started her heavy-bag routine. When she had more time, she preferred running, preferred that ache in her chest and the sting of the cold autumn air. But the heavy bag was a great way to tire herself out in a short amount of time.

She let the music pound in her ears, let her heart rate skyrocket, let her fists fly. All she felt was the pop of her gloves against the bag. That was all she'd let herself feel.

When it was done, when the sweat was dripping down her face as she headed for the shower, she still couldn't hide from the truth. As much as she'd tried to stay indifferent to Bridget, she wasn't. She couldn't be. There was too much unfinished business left between them to be ignored.

What the hell was she going to do about it, then?

She shed her workout clothes on the way up the stairs and dropped them in the laundry basket in the corner of the second-floor hall. Then she slipped into the shower, making sure the spray wasn't too hot. She should be exhausted, but she felt like she could run a good ten miles right now and still not wear off all this excess energy.

Sighing, she worked up a lather with the soap and washed off the layer of sweat. If she scrubbed hard enough, maybe she'd wash off all the regret and uncertainty she carried.

She soaped up her hair next, working her fingers through her locks. This had been her way of life—keep her hands busy to keep her head busy. For years, she'd been able to pretend that was enough.

Here, standing in this shower, she knew Lu was right. She had to let go. Her hands had been cramped, and so had her heart. She needed to let go in order to breathe easier, laugh easier, love easier.

The thing she had to let go of wasn't about Bridget, though. It wasn't the ability to care for another person, to see the best in them, to lower her defenses and let them inside. It was none of that.

The thing she had to let go of was her anger, this monster that had been perched on her back all this time, preventing her from opening up. Her anger was a sullen, hateful thing born of all the pain she hadn't been able to deal with, the heartache. Born of the truth she hadn't wanted to face—that she shared the blame in this mess.

It was time, though. If she carried this anger any longer, she would lose out on so much of her life. She would never know what it was to love again, to be happy again.

So, as the shower washed away the soap on her skin, she willed her anger to go with it, to swirl down the drain and leave her in peace. Maybe, just maybe, she would be able to pick herself up and get on with her life.

In the back of the fire hall, a folding table held refreshments, mostly cookies and punch. Rows of metal folding chairs faced two tables with white plastic tablecloths over them. In the center sat June Withershaw, the mayor. The rest Bridget didn't recognize. Probably city officials.

After they'd helped themselves to punch and cookies, Evelyn led them to a trio of middle chairs a few rows from the front.

An older woman named Mrs. Yackovich leaned around Evelyn to say, "Why, Bridget, how nice to see you again. It's been so long!"

Bridget's smile was strained. The woman didn't mean anything by it, didn't mean to call her out on not coming back for so long, but she still felt the sting of it, the underlying accusation that she hadn't done enough for this town. "Hi, Mrs. Yackovich. How are you?"

"Same old creaks in my joints! Congratulations on all your success."

"Thank you. This is my friend, Max."

"Ooh, what a handsome fellow. Are you two dating?"

Max laughed.

Bridget colored. "No. We write songs together."

"Ohhh. Making music so often leads to making other things."

Bridget sank lower in her seat as Evelyn changed the subject. Even if she were interested in Max like that, it didn't matter while she was still hung up on her ex. That was why her relationship with Patrick had fallen apart. She groaned. As much as she wanted to stay and see Alex every day, feel that sweet ache that came with their interactions, maybe she should cut this trip short.

Max leaned over to murmur, "I think I should get a shirt that says, 'I'm just the best friend.'"

"Honestly, not sure that would help."

"You know what would?"

Don't say it. Don't say it. Don't say it.

"Actually dating someone," Max said, putting enough emphasis on the last word to communicate that by 'someone,' he meant 'Alex.'

God, could everyone just shut up and leave them alone? This situation was hard enough without unsolicited advice. She elbowed him in the side, hard enough to shut him up until June got the meeting going. They discussed how Craft Street tended to flood when the rains increased, the budget for fixing potholes, and the impending teacher strike. That topic put a crease in Bridget's forehead. It was ridiculous that teachers got paid a pittance and, on top of that, were expected to buy supplies for their classrooms. How were they supposed to get any teaching done when they were stressed out by finances? If only she could do more than pay for a new roof for the school. Maybe she should anonymously contribute to a teachers' fund? That wouldn't solve the underlying problem, though. For that, the money would have to be a constant pool and come from the city.

"Now, on to the fall festival," June said.

The crowd stirred, like this was what they'd been waiting for, a chance to talk about the biggest event of the year.

"I'm sure many of you have heard the bad news," June said. "The festival hired Last Chance to play at the concert. However, the Chance siblings were in an ATV accident this past weekend. They'll be fine, but they're in the hospital if anyone would like to pay them a visit or send them well wishes. Obviously, though, that leaves the band without half its members and therefore us without a band. So, if anyone has any suggestions, let's hear them."

Murmurings arose as people discussed options.

Then an older gentleman raised his hand and said, "What about the church choir?"

Bridget snorted and, judging by the answering boos, more people were on her side than his.

"That's a lovely suggestion, Tom, but people can hear the choir every Sunday. We're interested in showcasing local talent that doesn't have a weekly place to perform," June said.

"Not to mention we want an act that will draw a crowd," someone added.

The silence was broken by whispering as people thought aloud or conversed with their neighbors.

Max leaned over again. "You want to contribute to the town? This seems like a pretty good opportunity."

As soon as he said it, Bridget knew it was the right thing to do. She studied his eyes, so sincere. "I'd need you with me." She'd performed without him, loads of times, and on tour, she performed with a full band, too. She'd just prefer not to be alone on the stage, not for her first concert in her hometown since she'd made it big.

"And I'll be there."

She took a deep breath, ignored the way her palms were sweating and her heart was racing. He was right. Alex and all their friends were right, too. She hadn't given back enough, not to this place that was so dear to her heart. This would be a big chance to show that she still cared, to show that she wasn't so famous that she'd forgotten about the people who'd raised her and nurtured her talent.

And maybe, along the way, she'd be able to prove something to Alex, too. Was it still a good deed if you were doing it to prove that you were a good person? But she didn't care if the entire town thought she was a good person. The only person whose opinion she cared about was Alex.

She raised her hand. June indicated that she could speak.

Bridget stood, pressing shaky hands against her thighs. "I know the festival is supposed to showcase younger talent, but this festival, this town, gave me my start, and I'd love to give back. If the council agrees, I would be happy to perform."

Later that night, as Bridget lay awake in bed, her phone buzzed with a single text message:

It wasn't you I've been mad at all these years.

For the first time since their post-dinner conversation, her heart unclenched.

Chapter Eight

Then

BRIDGET FIXED THEM CUPS OF tea while Alex sat on the couch, going over their calendars and budget. This weekly meeting kept them both on track and ensured they didn't overspend on trivial things, so they could pay their rent and student loans. Even with their tight budget, they had no savings to speak of.

Having to think about money all the time was exhausting, and Bridget felt it in her bones. She tossed the teabags out and crossed into the living room.

Alex accepted her mug with a tired smile. "Thank you. Did you get Saturday off?"

"Uh…" Bridget sat down on Benny's other side and gave him a good ear-scratching. "Saturday…"

"It's my dad's birthday dinner. Remember?"

"Oh. Right. God, I thought that was next weekend." Sighing, Bridget rubbed her eyes. "I'll see if I can switch with Jackie."

"Thanks. I know he'll be happy to see you," Alex said.

Bridget would be happy to see him, too. He had a gentle heart, and she was so grateful that he loved and approved of her, just as her own mom loved and approved of Alex. They were lucky that way. Lucky in a lot of ways, but especially that one.

Alex set her tea on the coffee table and peered at her spreadsheet. "I think we should reduce our grocery budget."

"By how much?" Bridget asked as she ran a hand down Benny's side. He leaned into the touch. He was such a good dog.

"Mm." Alex tilted her head. "Maybe ten dollars a week? That should lessen the squeeze for utilities every month."

That would mean even more cheap meals of noodles or peanut butter and jelly sandwiches. Tasty every once in a while. Every day—not so much. Maybe Bridget could pick up an extra shift at the diner every other week. That could help cover the groceries.

Alex scratched Benny's ears. "We rushed into adopting you, didn't we, boy?"

Bridget felt a twinge of guilt. She was the one who'd pushed to bring him home. Now, they had to add dog food and vet bills to the budget. Thank God Alex was decent with money. Bridget was always too tired to calculate which cereal in the massive aisle was the best deal.

"I could pick up more freelancing," Alex said.

"Babe, what? No." Bridget reached over Benny to rub the back of Alex's neck. "You already work so hard."

She took a sip of tea and pursed her lips. There was a simple solution here. Even though it wasn't one Bridget relished, *she* wasn't the one who'd be the major roadblock.

"We'll be home this weekend," she said. "We can always ask our parents to help with rent next month or even two months. It can be our Christmas present. Ooh, we could go on a fancy date. We haven't been on a really nice date since before graduation."

Almost six months. She wasn't high maintenance when it came to dates. She loved walks in the park and watching meteor showers and evenings spent cuddling on the couch. But every once in a while, she liked to dress up for Alex. Her chest fluttered with anticipation. There was almost nothing she loved more than Alex in a suit.

Alex's jaw tightened, and Bridget saw the protest coming before she even opened her mouth.

"It's not the worst option in the world," Bridget said.

"It's not the best, either," Alex said.

"What do you want me to do? Get a third job?"

"I could get a second one."

"You already work over fifty hours a week."

"And you take care of the apartment and do most of the cooking."

"Only because you're working all the time."

Bridget set down her mug. She ran a hand through her hair and swiveled on the couch to face Alex. "They're our parents. They love us."

"I know they do, but we're adults. We're supposed to be able to do this on our own."

"We're six months out of college! It's okay if we don't have everything figured out yet. Isn't that what you're always saying?"

"That's different."

"Why? Because it's me?" Bridget's voice rose, though it wasn't Alex she was upset with. "I'm allowed to take time to get my career off the ground, but you have to be superwoman? That doesn't make sense. You don't have to be so damn hard on yourself all the time."

Nestled between them, Benny looked back and forth a few times before jumping off the couch and padding into the bedroom away from the argument.

When Alex didn't reply, Bridget said, "I don't get why you're too proud to ask for a little help."

"Because I don't want to burden my dad any more than I have already. You wouldn't understand."

Alex's dad, Bridget knew, had used the majority of his savings to help send Alex to school, to let her come out with a little less debt than normal.

"Alex," Bridget said as Alex set her laptop on the coffee table and got up to go to the kitchen.

She did this. Ran away from conversations that veered too close to confrontations. Alex finished her tea, rinsed out the mug, and put it in the dishwasher. Then she disappeared into the bedroom.

Bridget sighed. She followed and found Alex in the bathroom, brushing her teeth. Bridget hugged her from behind, gauging Alex's expression in the mirror.

"Why don't I just ask my mom for a bit? You know she's happy to help, and it wouldn't burden your dad," she said against Alex's neck.

Alex leaned down to spit out toothpaste. "I just don't want them to worry about us. I want them to see us as adults."

This wasn't what Bridget imagined their post-college life would look like—always struggling to stick to their budget, never building up any savings, and too frequently too tired from work to have meaningful disagreements. Undoubtedly, it wasn't what Alex had imagined, either.

They were partners, though, and that meant sticking together through feast *and* famine.

She gave Alex a gentle squeeze. "Sometimes being an adult means knowing when to ask for help."

In the reflection, Alex found Bridget's gaze. "Okay. I'll think about asking my dad for a little bit, too."

"Thank you," Bridget said. She kissed Alex's cheek. "That's all I ask."

Most likely, once Bridget asked her own mom, they wouldn't need any help from Alex's dad anyway.

"I believe you when you say we'll get there," Bridget continued. "Do you believe it?"

Alex relaxed back into Bridget's embrace. She nodded, and Bridget squeezed her a little bit tighter.

Now

Grasping a bundle of chrysanthemums in one hand, Alex walked through the stiff grass in the graveyard. When she reached her parents' graves, she kneeled and placed the flowers between the two stones. It was kind of silly, bringing living flowers for the dead. Her mom had loved them, though, and her dad had loved her mom.

"Hey, Mom. Hey, Dad," she said quietly. "I'm sorry it's been a little while. Things have been…interesting. You probably know Bridget's back in town. You probably also know I've had a hard time dealing with it. I just wanted to say, Pop, that you were right. I was holding onto my anger so tightly I couldn't even see anything else. It's going to take me some time to fully let go, but I'm trying. That's the important thing, right?"

She sighed, squinting into the mid-morning sun. "I feel…nervous. I don't think I want things to go back to how they were, but I'm not sure how I want them to change. What should I do? If you were here now, what would you tell me?"

Although she wished her parents were still around to help her through times like this, it wasn't the answer that was helpful. It was the asking and letting herself think about it. What did she want to happen with Bridget?

Maybe she shouldn't have any expectations at all, just see how things shook out.

She sat with them for a while, just thinking and wishing they were here. But they were still with her in a way, in the way that mattered, and she took heart in that.

All too soon, though, it was time to head back to work. She patted her thighs. "Sorry, but I have to go. I love you both. I'll come again soon." She brushed two fingers against her lips and then touched her parents' names in turn. Calvin and Georgia Marlow. If she could grow up to be half the people they were, she'd be lucky. Some days, she thought she was getting there. Other days, not so much.

She walked back to her truck but stopped when she spotted someone standing near it, their back to her. The knit hat didn't hide that golden hair.

"Bridget?" Alex asked, coming closer.

"I'm sorry," Bridget said as she turned around. "I wasn't eavesdropping or anything. I didn't even know you were here."

"Oh." Alex shuffled. "Are you visiting your dad?" Mr. Callahan was buried not too far away from this section.

"Already did, actually."

Alex indicated the flowers in Bridget's fist. "Did you forget to leave those?"

Bridget shook her head. "No. They're, um, they're for your parents. I wanted to say hi."

Hot tears pressed against Alex's eyes. She had to take a deep breath to get her voice under control. "That's really nice of you." She stepped aside to let Bridget pass.

"Okay. See you around, Alex."

"Yeah, see you."

Alex got into her truck but couldn't help watching Bridget as she walked through the headstones. She'd told her parents that she was trying. Was this a chance to do that? To prove that she was a bigger person today than she was yesterday?

She started the engine, plugged in her phone, and synced up a podcast. Out of the corner of her eye, she watched Bridget. If she was done in the next couple minutes, Alex would offer her a ride back to town. That couldn't be so bad, right?

"Get it together, Alex," she murmured, tapping the steering wheel.

Without the simmering anger she'd nurtured for so long, would she even know how to interact with Bridget?

Too soon, Bridget turned away from the gravestones and walked back toward the road.

Alex rolled down her window. "Are you going my way?"

Bridget's expression hovered between pleasantly surprised and skeptical. "Are you sure?"

"Yeah. Hop in."

They rode in silence for a few minutes. It was different than the last time Alex had driven her, though. Less tense and more...sad.

Alex adjusted her grip on the steering wheel. This was it. Time to woman up.

"We, uh..." She cleared her throat. "We have open mic night once or twice a month, and it's this week. Tonight, actually."

"That sounds cool."

"You should come by. You and Max. I bet people would like to hear you play."

"Really?"

"Of course."

Bridget was quiet for a moment. Then she said, "Look, Alex, I don't want to ruin this moment, but you've wanted nothing to do with me since I got back, and now you're..." She gestured at Alex, at a loss for words.

"Giving you a ride and inviting you to hang out in my bar?"

"Yeah!"

Alex smiled, soft and sad. At least she was driving so she could keep her eyes on the road. "I've been thinking about what you said about being friends. I think I'm ready to try. If you're willing, that is."

"Yeah, absolutely," came Bridget's quick and breathy answer.

"Okay."

"Okay."

"Want me to drop you off at home?"

"Actually, if you're going into town, would you mind dropping me off at the café? I'm meeting Owen for lunch."

Alex shouldn't ask. It was none of her business. But the question came out anyway. "You are?"

Bridget's cheeks colored, like she was embarrassed to talk about it. "We're going to talk about the festival since he runs the tech. And because he's home with the baby most of the time, I figured he might want to get out of the house for a bit."

"Oh. Are you helping out?"

It would be good for Bridget to get involved with the town. So many people had loved her even before she'd shot to fame, and now they loved having her back. If she participated in the festival, showed pride in her hometown? Even better.

Alex squirmed as she felt Bridget's gaze on her. "What?" she asked.

"Did anyone tell you what happened at the town hall meeting last night?" Bridget's tone was cautious.

Alex adjusted her grip on the steering wheel. It figured that the one meeting she missed in ages was the one with a bombshell. Hopefully a good one, though? "No, no one told me anything." Her friends hadn't returned to the bar after the meeting. They hadn't even texted to give her a heads-up about whatever this was.

"Oh, um…"

Alex chanced a glance. Bridget sounded worried. "Is it that bad?"

That seemed to break through to Bridget. "Oh," she said, letting out her breath. "No, it's not bad at all. The band they hired had to back out, so, well, I'm going to do it."

Without warning, a wave of memories rushed over Alex. Years and years of fall festivals spent by Bridget's side. A handful of ones she hadn't.

She licked her lips. "That's great, Bridge."

Bridget brightened. "Really?"

"Really. Everyone's going to love it. They've been waiting for you to come back since you hit it big."

Bridget's smile faltered as Alex hung a right onto Main Street. "Right," she said.

Bridget sipped her coffee as they waited for Pippa's video call. Owen sat beside her, bouncing Keiko on his lap. Max sat on the other side of the table, pulling faces to make Keiko laugh. Bridget was nervous. Why was she nervous? She'd played in professional sports stadiums before. She could handle a concert in the park, surely.

But it was Alex. It was always Alex, wasn't it?

Bridget was nervous about performing in front of her, nervous about performing songs *about* Alex in front of Alex.

"I told her," she said.

"Hmm?" Owen licked the foam from his upper lip. "Told who about what?"

"Alex. That I'm doing the concert."

"Oh."

She exchanged a look with Max, who shrugged. "Oh?"

"Well, I thought you were going to say that you— Something else. I thought you were going to say something else," Owen said.

Bridget let it slide. "It's just that I thought it would make her happy somehow. She'd accused me of not caring about this place."

"Well," Owen said slowly, like he was choosing his words carefully, "are you doing this because you feel a responsibility to your hometown or because you want Alex to be proud of you?"

She sipped her coffee. Quietly, she asked, "Why can't it be both?"

Her video chat program chimed. She accepted the call, and her agent's face popped up on screen. "Hey, Pippa."

"Bridget!" Pippa said. "So good to see that you're alive even if you can't be bothered to answer my texts."

"I've been working. I swear," Bridget said, barely containing her eye roll. Pippa knew how hard she worked. She deserved a bit of a break. "Max is here, too. Say hi."

"Hey, Pip."

"Oh, good," Pippa said. "Then you're on board for this plan?"

"Absolutely," he said.

"We were thinking we'd do an acoustic show," Bridget said. "You know, something stripped down so it's just the two of us. Acoustic guitars, an amped piano if we can manage it."

"People are going to love that," Pippa said. "How big is the stage? Can you get a piano on it? Where's the piano coming from? What if it rains?"

"It's a covered stage," Owen offered.

"Yeah," Bridget confirmed. The piano was her main instrument, and she'd love to have one, but it wasn't like the town had one lying around, and the one at her mom's house was an old upright that had seen better days. To do the music justice, she'd prefer a baby grand. If she wanted one, she'd have to buy it herself, and then what would she do with it? Store it at her mom's house, where it wouldn't be used for another five years?

Pippa waved a hand dismissively. "I'll make some calls. What about exposure? How many people show up to this thing?"

"Probably a couple thousand," Owen said. "But that's over the course of the festival."

Bridget turned the screen to include him. "Pip, this is Owen. He does tech for the festival."

Pippa leaned closer. "Is that a baby?"

"Yeah!" Beaming, Owen raised Keiko's hand. "Say hi, Keiko!"

"Um, hello," Pippa said awkwardly.

Bridget hid her chuckle by taking a sip of coffee.

Pippa recovered from the interaction. "A couple thousand? Bridget, if you post about it just once online, I bet we can get ten times that size."

"Yeah, Pip, this town can't hold that many," Bridget said. "And the park certainly can't."

"What about streaming the concert live online?" Owen suggested. "You could charge a minimum amount for access or even make it free but leave it open for people to donate more. Half the proceeds could go to the town, half to you."

She didn't need half, but that was a detail they could hash out later. "That sounds incredible. I love that idea."

"So do I," Max agreed.

"Excellent. Get me the city council contact info, would you?" Pippa said.

"I'll get it to you," Owen said to Bridget.

"This is going to be amazing press, Bridget," Pippa said.

"That's not why I'm doing it."

"I know. I know. But half the world hates you for breaking up with Patrick, so you're in need of some good press, honey."

"Gee, thanks." She didn't need the reminder that she'd been fucking up her life at every turn.

"Oh, cheer up, sweetheart. You know I'm only looking out for you."

"Yeah, I know."

"Good. Then I'll be there on Wednesday. I love you both, but I don't trust you to find a way to set this up correctly."

Max scoffed. "Thank you for your faith in us."

"If we're going to do this, we're doing it right, Mister." Pippa pointed a finger at Bridget. "You two worry about the music. Let me worry about the rest."

"Thanks, Pip," Bridget said.

"Yeah, see you soon," Max added.

Pippa signed off.

Bridget took a long gulp of coffee. In the early days, her pain was what had kept her going—kept her writing songs and perfecting them and performing at dive bars and taking double shifts so she could scrape up enough money to pay rent. But Alex had been far away then, a distant, if depressing, memory.

How the hell was she supposed to play those songs with Alex so close?

Alex's invitation stuck in her mind. If she was so worried about playing in front of Alex in front of the entire town, why not do a test run?

Riley ran open mic night. She cared about bringing culture to the community, and she was better in front of people than Alex. After the first two or three weekly events, they'd run out of willing participants, so they'd moved to once or twice a month as they felt like it or as people asked for it. Nowadays, it was usually the same four who performed.

Jill, who read Shakespearean monologues, always themed to the month.

Zach, who'd played "Over the Rainbow" on his ukulele every single time until Alex and Riley bought him a book of new songs to learn. Now, he only played it every other month.

Brittany, a senior at the high school who read her poetry.

And Jamie, a seven-year-old whose specialty was tall tales with her own peculiar twists.

That was the usual lineup.

Tonight, when Bridget and Max walked in, each holding a guitar case, everyone immediately knew what they were up to. A shiver of excitement ran through the customers. Fresh blood, and famous blood, at that.

Riley nudged Alex. "Looks like they came prepared. A little presumptuous, don't you think?"

"No."

"No? That's all you're going to say?"

With a half-hearted shrug, not quite meeting Riley's eye, Alex said, "I invited them. I thought it'd be good for the community to get a glimpse of their beloved hometown girl."

"Won't they get that at the fall festival?"

"Sure, but they need to build excitement for the concert. Word-of-mouth and all that stuff."

"Huh."

Riley studied her intensely enough that Alex turned away. She busied herself with cutting up a lime. "Do you want to tell them they're on after Jamie?"

"Sure thing, Boss."

It wasn't until Riley got around the bar that Alex let out her breath.

Bridget sipped her water as Jamie finished her story, and the bar erupted with applause.

"You're good on the plan still?" Max asked.

Bridget nodded. "Yeah. Yep."

The plan could turn out to be very stupid, but she wouldn't know if she didn't try. Leave the ball in Alex's court. That was all she could do.

She followed Max to the small stage, where they unpacked their guitars and pulled up two stools. They did a quick tune-up, and then Bridget faced the crowd.

"Hi, everybody," she said, suddenly shy. "I'm Bridget."

"And I'm Max."

"Max is my writing partner. Some of you might have heard our stuff before."

Laughter ran through the bar.

"In the spirit of open mic night, though," Bridget continued, "we're not going to play you something you've heard before. We're going to try out something new. It's a song called 'When I Saw You Again.'"

"Feel free to tell us what you think afterward," Max said. "But if you hate it, at least be gentle."

Another titter of laughter.

He looked to her, silently asking if she was ready.

She nodded and counted them in. As soon as she strummed the first chord, she felt it—the peace that she found, without fail, in music. It centered her. Even with her anxiety over what she was about to do, the tension drained from her body. This was her safe space.

Alex bit her bottom lip. Hard. If she had thought *seeing* Bridget was bad, she'd never taken into account what hearing her sing would be like, how much it would hurt. Because Bridget used to sing to her like that. She used to sing in all different kinds of situations, of course. Making breakfast, shopping for groceries, tying her shoes, taking a shower.

But at home, in their apartment, Bridget would sing for *her*. She'd sing while they made dinner. She'd sing while she twirled Alex around the living room. She'd sing while they cleaned the apartment. She'd sing as they drifted off to sleep.

Alex straightened her spine. She didn't regret inviting Bridget to open mic night. She didn't.

But did she have to sing a song that hit so close to home? Did she have to sing a song that would remind everyone of what they used to be? This grief in Alex's heart was private, but the whole town could see it, had always been able to see it, like she wore it on her sleeve.

Jaw tight, she took the rag from her shoulder, set it on the counter, and disappeared out the back door into the alley. The night air was cool enough to sting, but she didn't button up her flannel. She just leaned against the brick wall and breathed slowly until her heartrate was somewhat under control.

So. Where did she go from here?

Most of the time, she powered through problems and kept working. Keeping her body busy was the best way to keep her head from running off in directions she didn't want it to go. Nights like these, though, maybe a few stiff drinks and a long sleep would help more than anything else.

The door lurched open. Bridget stepped out into the wan glow of the streetlight. Usually so confident, she looked uncertain, unsure of herself.

For a heartbeat, as Bridget walked toward her, she was seventeen again. She was seventeen and falling head over heels for her best friend instead of scrabbling to pull herself out of it.

For a heartbeat, she was twenty-three. She was twenty-three and wishing desperately for some explanation of how they'd fallen apart so completely.

For a heartbeat, she was twenty-five. She was twenty-five and signing up for dating sites in the hopes that she'd get over this constant ache but knowing that she never would. She was twenty-five, and she was trying, and why couldn't anyone see that?

Bridget gestured to the wall beside Alex. "Can I?"

Could she what? Lean against the wall?

Alex shrugged, and Bridget stood beside her, her back to the bricks. Was she thinking the same thing Alex was, about summer vacations when they'd come out here on Alex's breaks to make out? About how her dad had caught them more than once?

The memories made Alex's mouth go dry, her throat go tight. Because that song, those lyrics, said that Bridget still felt the way she had back then. Even through her haze of anger, Alex had known. It'd just been easier to hide from it.

But now that she acknowledged it, where did they go from here? It had taken so long to stitch her heart back together after the first breakup. What would she do when the second came? And it would. Because if Alex hadn't been good enough then, how could she possibly be good enough now? She pressed her palms to the brick wall behind her, the roughness grounding her.

"Did you like the song?" Bridget asked, her voice huskier than normal.

"It's not really something I could listen to objectively," Alex said. Why did she always have to be like this? Why couldn't she just say yes?

Bridget's silence meant all Alex could do was follow the spiraling in her head. No, she couldn't think about the song objectively, because all she could think about was —

"Was it about me?"

Bridget's gaze searched Alex's. Even in the yellow streetlight, her eyes were bright. Her chest heaved with words unsaid. Words about to be spoken?

"All of them are," she said, "in some way."

Alex gulped. Of all the answers she'd expected, that was the furthest from her mind.

Bridget shifted into Alex's space and whispered, "I can't write about anything but you."

Alex's heart sped into overdrive. She didn't want to be a muse. She just wanted to be good enough to come home to.

Bridget's eyes darted between Alex's. Then her gaze dropped to Alex's lips. She gave Alex ample time to pull away.

And yet…Alex didn't. She sucked in a breath as Bridget's lips met hers—softly, hesitantly, reverently. Bridget slid a hand to Alex's cheek, thumb stroking softly over her cheekbone. It was different, much different, than the desperate kiss they'd shared in her office. This kiss evoked memories of soft mornings spent wrapped around one another, quiet afternoons lazing on the couch watching TV.

Alex's heart filled to bursting. She could live in this moment.

If only she could let herself.

She pulled away slowly, breathing hard, loath to break the contact even though she needed to. She couldn't quite open her eyes. Not yet.

"I'll follow your lead," Bridget whispered.

Alex opened her eyes. Bridget's pupils were blown so wide the blue of her irises was barely visible. Alex itched to reach for her, but there would be no coming back from that. It was one thing to be kissed, quite another to initiate it. A jumble of emotions whirled in her chest. She couldn't think straight, not with Bridget so close.

"What do you want, Alex?" Bridget's breath puffed against her cheek.

She wanted them back. But she also wanted *not* to want that.

"I don't know," were the words that spilled from her lips.

Bridget dropped her hand from Alex's cheek and took a step back. "Okay," she said, nodding softly. "Okay."

So many thoughts raced through Alex's head that she didn't know which to voice first.

Are you sure?

Are you okay?

Am I okay?

Why do I still feel like this after all this time?

Bridget licked her lips, then ran two fingers over them. Her voice was still soft. "You're fine, Alex. It's fine. The last thing I want to do is pressure you. So, if you figure it out, let me know." She brushed a chaste kiss over Alex's cheek.

Alex was frozen.

Bridget offered one last, sad smile before going back inside.

Once again, Alex was left alone.

Chapter Nine

Then

"WE HAVE TO GO, BABY," Bridget said from the doorway, keeping her voice quiet, gentle.

Alex gave no indication that she'd heard. She sat at the edge of her childhood bed—forearms on her knees, shoulders hunched, head hanging. Her suit jacket lay on the back of her desk chair. Both it and the rest of her suit were pristinely pressed thanks to Evelyn, whose motherly instincts kicked into overdrive in a crisis.

Bridget stepped into the room, rested her hand on Alex's bowed shoulder, and squeezed.

"How am I supposed to do this?" Alex asked in a hoarse whisper.

Bridget sank onto the mattress and coaxed Alex into her arms. She'd felt much the same the day of her own dad's funeral, and Alex had been a big reason she'd gotten through.

"I'll be here. I'll be right here," she murmured, hoping it would be enough.

Alex wasn't a big crier, and she wasn't crying now, but her body felt slight, like she took up half the space she normally did. Bridget pulled her even closer. They could take a few more minutes. Then they had to go.

Bridget never let go of Alex's hand. She sat beside her at the funeral service, stood beside her as she said good-bye to her father for the last time, stayed close as they mingled with well-wishers. Bridget's mom had stepped in to take care of most of the preparations, including the catering for the funeral reception, which Alex walked through in a haze.

Bridget didn't know what to do beyond trying to be there for her.

As the reception wrapped up, Bridget helped clean up the kitchen until her mom rubbed her back and said, "Take Alex back to our house. I'm sure she's exhausted."

Along with her mom, her brothers and sister-in-law stayed to clean up, so when they got back to the Callahan house, it was quiet. Bridget turned on low lights as they made their way to her bedroom. They'd barely spoken all day. Bridget didn't know what Alex needed. So she asked.

Alex hesitated in the doorway to Bridget's room for a moment before saying, "I need to go for a run."

Oh. Whatever Bridget had expected, it wasn't that. But Alex was already moving, faster than she'd moved all day, grabbing her shorts and sports bra from the duffel bag in the corner and heading to the bathroom to change. Before Bridget could remind her that it was dark, that a run could wait til the morning, she was out the door.

Bridget changed into pajama pants and an oversized T-shirt, lay on her bed, and stared at the ceiling. She'd spent so much of the past few days consoling Alex, or trying to, that she hadn't yet processed her own feelings, and they came pouring out now. She sobbed for the loss of a man who'd been practically another father. And yet the whole while, she knew Alex's pain was a thousand times worse.

When she'd cried herself out, Bridget wiped her eyes as well as she could and checked her phone. An hour had passed. No calls or texts. She rubbed her eyes. Alex should've been back by now.

Bridget hurried out of bed, down the stairs, and out the patio door. Sure enough, Alex, still in her running outfit and probably freezing in the spring night, lay sprawled in the grass. Her chest heaved, though from exertion or with sobs, Bridget couldn't tell.

She ducked back inside to grab a blanket from the hall closet before going to Alex, who didn't say a word. But she let Bridget drape the blanket over her and lie down beside her and take her hand.

They gazed at the stars, and Alex held onto Bridget's hand like it was a lifeline as she cried.

Now

When Sunday dinner rolled around this week, Bridget was the one to open the door for Alex. She took the six-pack from Alex's hands with a smile. This was new. This was fine. Or it would be fine once Bridget figured out how to act. Because Bridget's heart still jumped into her throat every time she looked at her, but Alex didn't want anything more.

Dinner, at least, went better than the first time. The conversation flowed smoothly without Bridget having to contribute much. She pushed food around her plate and spent the majority of her time watching Alex.

Not in a creepy way, of course. Just in a way that made her ache from deep in her chest for what used to be, for what could have been.

The more she watched, though, the less she thought about Alex holding her and the more she thought about how grateful she was just for Alex's presence. Alex got along with every single person in this family. Arya and Dev especially adored her. And Alex had been here when Bridget hadn't been.

Alex held up this family, and she held up this town. Bridget was lucky to love her at all.

Alex loaded her hands with plates and followed Evelyn into the kitchen, where she cleared them off and loaded them into the dishwasher.

Evelyn smiled at her. "I'd say you don't have to do that, sweetheart, but I've told you enough times, haven't I?"

Alex nodded.

Evelyn hung up the towel she'd used to dry her hands and leaned her hip against the counter. "It's nice to see you and Bridget interact civilly again. A far cry from what it used to be, but I'm happy you've made progress."

Alex tried for a smile, but only the corner of her lips lifted. It was true that being in the same room as Bridget without needing to go a few rounds with her heavy bag was a pleasant change, a good one, but she still had no clue how to deal with their unfinished business.

Evelyn touched her shoulder. "Sweetie, is everything all right?"

Alex turned to face Evelyn, twisting her lips as she mulled over a request. She had every right to ask. She just didn't want Evelyn to read into it too much. Actually, to read into it at all. It didn't mean anything. It was just her trying to satisfy her curiosity.

"Actually," she said, "do you remember the CDs you said you were saving for me?"

"Of course."

"I was, uh, I was wondering if I could claim them now. I know it's been a long time, but—"

"Stop. You don't have to say anything more," Evelyn said. "I'll put them in a bag with leftovers for you."

So no one had to know.

Alex's throat tightened. But she only nodded and whispered, "Thank you," and closed her eyes as Evelyn pressed her lips to her forehead.

Bridget lifted her glass of wine to her lips and endeavored to keep her leg from bouncing up and down. Alex had disappeared onto the back patio ten minutes ago, and Bridget could barely contain herself.

Max shoved her knee.

"What?" she asked, turning her attention to him. "What was that for?"

"You're not even listening," he said. "We're talking about the show on Saturday."

"Oh. Right. What about it?"

"Owen's idea about livestreaming it for a dollar but asking for larger donations. I like it because it makes it more accessible, but it also doesn't ask for only a buck from people who would be willing to give more."

It was a genius idea, and she was happy to be part of it, happy to be able to help the school, the teachers, and the town.

A few minutes later, when Bridget had once again drifted out of the conversation, Evelyn put her hand on her knee and murmured, "You look like you have something else on your mind, something other than the concert."

Bridget smiled bashfully.

"Go to her. I think you two need to talk."

Bridget downed the last of her wine—much-needed liquid courage—set down the glass, and left the living room, snatching a blanket hanging over the armchair on the way. She paused in front of the patio door. Outside, Alex sat on the swing, forearms on her legs as she leaned forward. Her curly hair was loose today, the way Bridget loved it best. She used to like to play with it as they watched movies on the couch.

Maybe Bridget shouldn't go out there. Maybe she shouldn't force her presence on Alex when Alex clearly wanted a few minutes to herself.

Bridget fidgeted with the blanket in her hands. Okay, that was her in. She'd go and give it to Alex and, if Alex seemed interested in talking, she'd stay. There. A plan.

Alex looked over her shoulder when Bridget opened the patio door. It wasn't a look that demanded she go away. That was a start.

Bridget's heart pounded as she offered the blanket. "I thought you might be cold."

Alex gave a half smile as she draped the blanket over her shoulders. "Thank you."

Bridget clapped her hands together to cover the cracking of her heart. Alex didn't want her company. Alex didn't want *her*. "Okay, well…"

Alex slid over on the swing.

It was an opening. A small, silent one, but more than she'd had a second ago.

She seized it, careful to sit as far away from Alex as possible so as not to spook her. Even so, Alex draped the blanket over Bridget's shoulders, too, so they shared it. Bridget's heartrate hadn't come down yet. If anything, it had increased. Being this close to Alex without being able to reach out and touch her was miserable. How could she ever have given this up? What a damned fool she'd been.

"We need to talk," Alex said, voice soft.

Bridget blinked. Was this the part where Alex asked her to leave town? She wouldn't be wrong to do it. Alex had given so much to this town, and Bridget hadn't even thought about giving back until someone had told her to. If Alex didn't want her around, she would go.

Alex's shoulders shook as she breathed in and out deeply. "That night at the theater, we, uh, we left a lot of things unsaid."

Bridget nodded, hardly breathing, hardly letting herself hope. Alex had cut that conversation short, but here she was opening it up again.

"You said something that made me question how I'd been looking at things all this time. You, uh…" Alex cleared her throat. "You told me you'd give up your career to take back your decision."

Bridget didn't have to ask for clarification on which decision Alex meant. She'd tried not to think much about that night, instead focusing on the future—on music and writing and the fall festival. Along the way, she'd pushed out memories of what had happened in Alex's office, the kiss that had left her knees weak and her body aching for the ghost of what might have been.

Her chest tightened. This was the moment she'd been dreading since she came home, the moment she'd have to explain herself. She didn't want to hurt Alex any more than she already had. "I told you. I was young and stupid. Of course I regret it."

"That's not an explanation."

No, it wasn't, and Alex deserved an explanation. Bridget bit her lip. Alex probably couldn't hate her any more than she already did.

"I know I wasn't in the best state of mind," Alex said, her voice dangerously close to breaking, "but I guess I just can't understand why you gave up on something so great unless…unless you didn't think it was good."

Bridget shook her head. "That's not it at all. Most of the time, we were fantastic together."

"Then you fell out of love with me? Because I couldn't give you what you wanted, or…?"

"No, no, no." Bridget swiped a hand through her hair and swallowed thickly. "I didn't do it because I didn't love you anymore. I did it *because* I loved you."

Alex's brow creased. "What? You thought leaving me would somehow benefit me?"

Oh, this wasn't going well at all. Hearing it out loud made Bridget cringe. She sighed, thinking back to the moment she made the stupidest and most well-intentioned decision of her life. All that had been in her mind was that she couldn't keep doing the same thing day in and day out, couldn't see how things would change unless she forced them to.

She hung her head in her hands and rubbed her face. "I didn't know what else to do," she finally said. "We weren't... We were just broken, and I couldn't figure out how to fix us. So I tried to force it, but I did it in the worst possible way."

Alex stared at the ground.

Bridget didn't blame her. What could anyone say to that? But not all of the blame belonged to her. "For the longest time, I could imagine a future with you. It was just a given. But all of a sudden, I couldn't imagine it anymore."

Her voice cracked on the last word. A flash of a future that she'd dreamed of but never was—where they said their vows in front of their closest family and hosted holidays at their home and fell asleep with their hands intertwined, their rings clinking against one another. She ached for what could have been. She ached for what their youthfully stupid selves had thrown away so callously.

Alex still hadn't replied. Instead, she'd buried her head in her hands.

Bridget took a deep, shaky breath. At least Alex wasn't running away, and that meant she had to say all the hard things they agreed on saying. "You told me you didn't get the job." And even though Alex didn't need the details, she added, "That interpreting job in D.C. that you'd interviewed three times for, the one that was pretty much the only thing you'd been excited about in months. You turned it down, and then you lied to me about it."

Alex frowned, but she didn't reply.

It was answer enough.

"That's when I knew," Bridget said. "That's when I knew we couldn't keep on like we were. You lied about that job, and maybe you didn't exactly lie about selling your dad's business, but at some point, you stopped planning on that and didn't acknowledge it." She wanted to cry. She breathed deeply until the urge passed, at least for now. What she would give to go back to that day and handle things differently. "When did we start lying to each other?"

Alex, like always, was stoic to the point of being emotionless. "So, you left me? That wasn't a very smart plan."

"I was twenty-three. Everything I did was dumb," Bridget said. "But at least I had a plan. You weren't making any decisions at all. Something needed to change, and you refused to even talk about it. What choice did you give me?"

She stood up, letting the blanket flutter onto the swing. She needed distance from Alex, from that blank expression that infuriated Bridget more than anything. It was like she didn't even care.

As the frustration flared up, she leaned her bum against the railing and crossed her arms. "And I didn't leave *you*. I left the situation. I'm not the one who didn't pick up my phone for a year, remember?"

Alex deflated. "Right. So, it's all my fault. That's what it always comes back to, isn't it?"

Oh, shit. Bridget had just made everything worse. What Alex needed wasn't anger and accusations. It was understanding. Understanding that they'd both fucked up and that they both needed to change. "No, Alex..."

"I know I shut down. I know I shut you out. And I know it wasn't fair to you," Alex said. "But can you honestly tell me you did it for me? To knock some sense into me and not because of any selfish reasons? Because from where I'm standing, as soon as you ditched me, your life took an upturn, and if you really wanted to fix us, somehow I don't think me not picking up the phone would've stopped you."

Bridget's first instinct was to deny, to protest, but she fought that. The slight hesitation was enough for the realization to sink in. She'd given up on them, and she'd left Alex behind.

"No," Bridget said, "I guess not."

"I need to go," Alex said, heading down the back porch steps and toward the side of the house to bypass everyone sitting inside.

Bridget walked after her. "What? Alex, wait."

"Apologize to your family for me."

"Alex, please don't do this. Please don't run away again." Bridget's voice was thick with emotion because this was what Alex did. She ran. And yes, they both shared the blame, but how were they ever going to move past it if they couldn't face it, no matter how scary it was? "I know it's hard, but if we try, we can get past this."

Alex stopped. She didn't turn around, but she stopped. Sniffling, she brought her hands to her face, and her voice was muffled when she said, "Can we? I pushed you away—so far away that you went to a different state so you didn't have to deal with me."

Bridget bit her lip. Hard. If she wasn't careful, she'd start crying, too, and if she started, she might never stop. "You were in pain."

"So were you." When Alex turned, there were no tearstains on her cheeks.

Bridget nodded. "Yeah, I was, and our pain got in the way of us being able to give each other what we needed, and that's no one's fault."

"Isn't it?" Alex chuckled mirthlessly. "I was the one who pushed you away. I was the one who could never talk about it. I was the one who blamed you for giving up on me. I was the one who didn't pick up the phone after you left." Her voice was even softer when she added, "And I've been running from that all this time. How is that not my fault?"

All Bridget wanted to do was hold Alex, hold her tight until the tears came and went and all their hurt went with them. But Alex needed her space more than Bridget needed her touch. So she said, "There's no shame in the truth, Alex. We loved each other, but we were young, and we let all the things that stressed us out and hurt us get in the way, and we lost sight of what mattered most—each other."

Alex took a moment to absorb her words. She stuffed her hands in the pockets of her jeans, hunched her shoulders against the chill. Finally, her brown eyes met Bridget's. "I'm sorry. I'm sorry for the part I played, for all the pain I caused you. I'm so sorry."

Bridget let the tears that had been threatening fall now. Fuck, did this hurt, like cleaning glass out of a wound before it could heal. The pain was necessary, but that didn't make it any less excruciating.

Alex gestured vaguely toward the street. "I need to go."

Nodding, Bridget followed her around the side of the house to where her truck was parked at the curb.

"Thank you for being honest with me," Alex said.

She hopped in and barely got buckled up before pulling away, leaving Bridget standing on the sidewalk, feeling completely useless. Bridget watched the truck until it turned the corner. No matter what she did to try to make things better, she only ended up making them worse. At least it was out in the open now. No more hiding from the pain they'd caused each other. No more hiding from the blame. Maybe now they could finally move forward.

If Alex ever wanted to talk to her again.

Alex didn't even get to the intersection before the tears started, and once they started, it quickly became a deluge. She turned the corner and pulled over, unbuckling as the sobs started, fast and violent.

Shame ricocheted through her. Bridget *did* blame her. If only she hadn't been depressed. If only she hadn't been so emotionally stunted that she couldn't have a proper conversation. If only she had picked up the phone after the breakup. That was all it would have taken. But no, she'd let her pain—over her dad's death, over the split—cloud her judgment.

What an absolute mess she'd made of her life.

Bridget's question from the other night echoed in her mind.

What do you want?

What *did* she want? The only way she could move forward was if she figured that out, but nothing had ever terrified her so much.

Chapter Ten

Then

As Alex left her supervisor's office, she sent Bridget a quick text telling her not to wait up. Like so many days over the past few months, she'd go straight to the café after her shift here. At first, it had been a way to stay close to her dad. But now, seven weeks out from his death, it was about the work. The work was the only thing that kept her mind busy, kept it off how empty she felt all the time.

She sank into her desk chair and pulled on her headphones. That was the worst part—the emptiness. Right after it happened, she'd wake up with an ache in her chest like someone had cut her open during the night. Now, she worked a lot. She slept a lot. She drank a lot. At least it made the pain go away. It was the only way she knew how to get through it.

But in two weeks, it would get better. She wouldn't have to do all this back-and-forth anymore and would be able to devote herself full-time to the business her dad had loved. Not that Bridget would be happy about the new arrangement. Alex knew she was worried, but they just had to be patient. This would blow over in a few months, wouldn't it?

Her phone buzzed. Bridget had texted back a quick, emotionless, "Okay."

Alex ignored all the other notifications—a plethora of texts, some missed calls, even a handful of voicemails. She didn't want to talk to anyone.

When she arrived at the apartment after closing up the cafe, her eyes were tired and her feet were heavy. Good. That meant she could fall into bed and not care about anything. She was just marking time until the day she could feel something again. Now that she was armed with an action plan, she hoped that day would be sooner rather than later.

She found a plate of chicken and potatoes in the microwave. After warming it, she dropped onto the couch to eat. Benny padded out into the living room to keep her company as she ate, lying on her feet. She turned on the news in the background but barely paid attention. So Bridget had gone to bed without her. She'd both wished for that and feared it. She had to tell Bridget eventually. And if Bridget didn't want to move back home, well, they could do long distance. It was only an hour. They could make it work.

And she could make Bridget understand that her dad had left the café to her, that the assistant manager could only act as the unofficial manager for so long, that decisions had to be made and Alex was the one who had to make them.

She knew that now, even though at the beginning, a part of her had thought that if she never addressed it, it'd never be real, not entirely. Now, she hated that it meant he was really gone, but still, she would carry on his legacy.

She let out a long breath, turned off the TV, and got up to load her plate into the dishwasher. She opened a bottle of beer and, leaning against the counter, gulped a third of it down.

Oh, God. Tears pricked at her eyes. Her mom had died when she was so little that she hadn't properly understood. But this wound was still fresh. She held her breath to hold back the tears.

But she couldn't hold her breath forever.

She took another fortifying sip of beer, swallowing the rock in her throat at the same time, and went into the bedroom, where she got ready and slipped into bed beside Bridget, who was fast asleep. Benny jumped up, too, and settled at the bottom of the mattress.

Even in the darkness, Bridget's golden hair haloed her head. When Alex brushed a lock behind her ear, Bridget moved into the touch and stirred awake.

Alex sighed. Would she want to come along?

"Hey, baby," Bridget murmured. She curled into Alex, tiredly burrowing into her neck and snaking an arm around her waist.

"Hey," Alex said. "Sorry I woke you."

"S'okay."

Biting her bottom lip, Alex ran her fingers up and down Bridget's arm. The more she put this off, the harder it would get. "Since you are, though—awake—I should tell you that my schedule should get easier soon."

Opening her eyes, Bridget shifted to look at Alex properly. "Does that mean you're stepping back from the café? Good. I've missed you."

"No. It means I put in my two weeks."

Bridget propped herself up on an elbow. "What? Why? I thought you were selling the café?"

"I still can. I might. But I want to experience it before I make a decision, and I don't want to do that hastily."

Bridget ran her fingers through her hair. "You don't want to make a hasty decision, but you quit your job to focus on a café that you're going to sell?"

"Might. I said I might sell it."

Bridget lay back against the pillows, farther away from Alex now.

Alex flipped on her side to face her. "What?"

"I don't know. You quitting your job seems like something we should've talked about, doesn't it?"

"I'm not asking you to move back home."

"Not yet."

Alex blinked in surprise. Could Bridget be that opposed to the idea? Lots of people commuted an hour to work. But it worked both ways. If it meant staying with Bridget, Alex would gladly drive an hour to and from the café each day.

"Then we won't move."

"And you'll never be here."

"Bridget..."

"It's not just that. Should you really have given up a steady job with health insurance? And what about that interview for the translating job? What if you get that? What then?"

Alex hadn't been able to think about that, really. That job was one her old self had wanted. It didn't seem so important now, but that didn't mean she'd discount it entirely. "I don't even know if I've made it past the first round of interviews yet. It's too early to take it into consideration."

"And when were you going to take me into consideration?" Bridget asked.

Alex reached out, but Bridget shifted her hand away. She'd thought Bridget would want what was best for her.

She pursed her lips. "You don't want to move back home, but you'd move to D.C. if I got that job?"

Bridget stared at the ceiling. A couple months ago, when Alex had applied, she wouldn't have even had to ask. But that was before her world had tilted on its axis. It scared her that she didn't know the answer now.

"I don't know. So much has changed since we first talked about it," Bridget said, rolling onto her side, away from Alex. "I have an early shift. We should talk about this another time."

"Yeah, okay." Alex stared at Bridget's back until her breathing evened out. Then she settled onto her back and closed her eyes, knowing whatever sleep she got tonight would be restless.

Now

Alex was two glasses of scotch deep when Jaya appeared at her door.

She held out a bag. "Evelyn asked me to drop these off for you. Leftovers."

"Right. Thank you." Alex brushed her hair out of her eyes and took the bag. "I'm sorry I ran out."

Jaya held up a hand. "No explanation necessary. Healing takes time. Just make sure you give yourself enough of it."

Alex nodded even though platitudes didn't get through to her anymore. Wasn't five years long enough? Jaya meant well, though, and Jaya loved her. That counted for something.

Jaya leaned forward to press a kiss to Alex's forehead. "Take care of yourself, okay? And maybe put down the bottle for tonight."

Alex looked up sharply—or as sharply as the alcohol coursing through her system would allow.

"You reek. It's coming out of your pores," Jaya said in answer to her unspoken question. "Ian and the kids are waiting in the car, so I have to go. Eat some leftovers and go to sleep early, okay?"

"Okay." Alex closed the door, closed herself inside her fortress of solitude, and took the leftovers to the kitchen. On top of the Tupperware containers sat two CDs, still wrapped in cellophane. There was a sticky note attached to each.

The one on Bridget's debut album read: *Alex, a lot of these songs say everything I couldn't put into words.*

But the second read only: *For Alex.*

Well, she was already drunk. Might as well get this over with. She put the leftovers in the fridge. In the living room, she sank onto the couch and poured herself another glass of scotch. She popped the debut CD into her laptop and studied the track list, which included "She," the song that, Alex remembered vaguely, had led to Bridget coming out as bi.

She let the album play through, her heart growing heavier with each track. Bridget's voice was a gift; she had always known that. But Alex found it particularly painful tonight.

By the middle of the fourth track, she was lying on the couch, staring up at the ceiling, tears trailing down her temples. Not that Bridget would lie about something like this, but she was right—every single song was about Alex in some way. Some were happy, the ones about first loves or summer kisses or belonging to someone so completely that they know everything about you. Alex recognized herself in the details—the kiss by the train tracks, stargazing on their first official date, the outfit she was wearing the first time Bridget told her she loved her.

The ones that weren't happy, well, it was easy to see the influence she had there, too. They were about taking blame, being sorry without knowing how to say it, losing something incredible. They were about being young and too stupid to know how to handle a relationship and the stresses that came with adulthood. They were about the color of the world fading once the person you loved was out of your life.

Together, the songs added up to an album that was essentially a love letter from Bridget to Alex. With that realization in her head, Alex fell asleep on the couch, still crying.

Bridget threw on a suit jacket over her sweater, smoothed it down, and checked her appearance in the mirror. With her jeans and sneakers, she looked respectable without being intimidating. She was going for small-town entrepreneur, not famous musician or big-city CEO.

Downstairs, she found Max in the kitchen, eating cereal.

"Well, well, well, don't you look nice and professional?" he said then narrowed his eyes. "What are you up to?"

"I have a meeting," she said breezily.

"With Pippa? You don't care about looking good for her."

Bridget studiously avoided his gaze as she grabbed a travel mug and filled it with coffee. "No. Um, it's not with her."

"Oh. Is it about the concert on Saturday?" Perking up, he half stood. "Should I get my jacket? I can even comb my hair."

She turned to face him. "It's not about the concert. It's not about music at all."

He settled back in his chair. "Well, if you want me to come, I can."

"Thanks, but this is something I have to do on my own."

He nodded and returned to his cereal. Then he asked, "Is it about Alex?"

Bridget sipped her coffee. "In a way."

"You know I'm here if you need to talk, right?"

Bridget smiled. "Of course I do. Thank you."

"Good luck with the meeting."

"Thanks. I'll be back in an hour or two to practice."

"Cool. I've got some ideas for 'On Stage.'"

"Can't wait to hear them. See you later."

Travel mug in hand, she donned her sunglasses and walked the few blocks down to Main and then up the street to the real estate office. The late October sun warmed her face, if not her heart.

The agency was located in a small corner building. The walls inside were painted a cool blue and featured framed photographs of bridges and vistas in the area.

Bridget approached the receptionist, a woman about her mom's age. "Hi. I have an appointment with Gina Gallo."

"All right, um…" She looked up and faltered, obviously caught off guard, as she reached for the computer mouse. She studied the screen, red blooming on her cheeks. "Let's see here. What—what's your last name?"

"Callahan."

"Why don't you have a seat, Ms. Callahan? Mrs. Gallo will be with you in a moment."

"Thank you." Bridget sat in the corner of the waiting room next to a table littered with magazines. She picked up a gossip magazine and flipped through it, stopping in surprise when she saw her own face staring back at her. Patrick's, too. It was a picture from a few months ago, when she'd attended a red carpet premiere with him. There was a cartoon tear drawn between their heads, and the headline read, "The Truth about Their Split."

Her mouth tasted sour. She wanted to look away but couldn't, not even when the article laid all the blame at her feet for not keeping Patrick satisfied.

"Ms. Callahan?"

Bridget snapped the magazine shut and put it back on the pile. Trying for a smile, she said, "Yes, that's me."

The woman standing in the hallway offered her hand. "Gina Gallo. A pleasure."

"Yes. Same."

"Follow me to my office."

The bare hallway was painted white, much less welcoming than the lobby. Gina's office, too, was rather plain. There was nothing on her desk except for her computer and a few silver picture frames. Her bookshelves were lined neatly with labeled binders. The only thing on the wall was a calendar.

"Please, take a seat," Gina said as she gestured to the chair in front of her desk and sat in the one behind it. She opened a folder, slipped glasses onto her nose, and consulted her papers. "Now, as I understand it, you're interested in the Wentworth Theater property?"

"That's right."

"May I ask why? It's an unusual request, and I like to know my clients' aims so as to best serve them."

Somehow, she doubted Gina would be interested in hearing that she and her ex-girlfriend used to sneak in there to daydream and make out. "It just… It holds a lot of memories for me. I hate going past it and seeing it all boarded up now."

"Yes. You're not the only one. At one point, the historical society expressed interest."

"What happened? Was it out of their price range?"

"No. Not exactly. The property is actually quite cheap, but repairs will be extensive. It's an investment property and likely won't see a return for a number of years." She smiled. "Not a purchase for the faint of heart.'

Bridget hesitated before replying. Was Gina trying to get her to back off? And if so, why? Shouldn't she want to make the sale? "I understand."

"It's just that, with someone such as yourself, who isn't in the area most of the time, are you really going to be able to update it properly?" Gina asked. "Someone will need to oversee the renovations."

"I hadn't really thought that far ahead," Bridget admitted. All she could think about was doing something nice for Alex—even if it had to be a parting gift. Because no, she couldn't stay. She had a life back in New York, not to mention a career that couldn't simply be put on hold. And there was no way she'd move on emotionally if she had to be *around* Alex all the time without getting to be *with* her.

"Well," Gina said, not unkindly, "perhaps it's time you start."

Weeknights at the bar were low-key, just how Alex liked. She served enough customers that she could go a little mindless while doing it, but it was never so busy that she got stressed. It was a nice balance.

Or it used to be.

She leaned her forearms on the bar top and took stock of the space. It was simple—wooden floors, wooden tables, wooden bar—and sparsely decorated. Just a place for people to come at the end of the workday to unwind. She'd never really made a conscious choice to stay. She'd only wanted to keep her dad's legacy alive. And she had. He was alive in the original café next door, in this bar, in the atmosphere of the town itself.

The emptiness eating her insides, though, was that because she'd given up on her professional aspirations to come home? Or was it because of the mistakes she'd made? Allowing Bridget to leave, holding that grudge until they were so far apart they couldn't find their way back to each other.

And now? Now, instead of wiping their slate clean and starting afresh, she had chosen to avoid Bridget, avoid the truth that she, too, shared the blame for how they came undone.

She was happy, wasn't she? Or she was the closest thing she could be to it. If she tried to chase happiness, could she expect to catch it? Moving to a new town, landing a new job, finding a new relationship—she wouldn't find her happiness there. But she'd made something for herself here, and she liked it. That was good enough. It had to be.

"Why don't you go take a break?" Riley said, sidling up beside her.

"Because it's not time for my break yet."

"Come on," Riley said. "It's slow enough that I can take care of things on my own. And if I need you, you'll be right in the corner hanging with your friends. Don't you trust me, Boss?"

"No, not really."

Riley smacked her with bar rag. "How rude. Go be mean to your friends instead."

Chuckling, Alex thanked her before heading to the corner table, where Owen, Jordan, and Lu were gathered. "Hi, guys," she said.

They greeted her with smiles, and Jordan nudged the empty chair out from the table. "Sit down for a few minutes, friend."

Alex obliged, dropping into the seat beside Lu. "Where's the tyke tonight?"

"It's Grandma's night with her," Jordan said.

Owen frowned. "I miss her."

"He gets separation anxiety, but don't worry. He'll be okay." Jordan squeezed her husband's hand, kissed him on the cheek, and turned back to Alex. "You getting ready for the festival?"

"Yeah. The brewery's got a booth."

"Speaking of," Lu said, casting a glance around, "where's our star and her little sidekick?"

Alex cleared her throat. "They're probably busy practicing for the concert."

"Good," Owen said. "I hope they play some new stuff."

"It's a good bet since her muse is right here," Jordan said.

"What's that supposed to mean?" Alex said, trying not to let her defenses fly up before it was warranted.

Jordan shrugged, too casual. "Just that you've been different the past few days, quieter. You're not spitting acid every time her name comes up anymore."

"But you two are also really good at pretending the other doesn't exist," Owen said.

"Until you think no one's looking," Lu added.

"What's going on? What's changed?" Owen asked.

"There's nothing going on." She couldn't explain it to her friends because she couldn't even explain it to herself.

The four of them were silent for a long, tense moment.

Alex tightened her jaw. She didn't need anyone sticking their nose in her business, even if they were her friends. Why couldn't they just leave her alone to figure things out?

Probably because she wouldn't figure them out. She'd just let things go without making a decision until something snapped—either Bridget left again or Bridget kissed her again. Why did decisions always paralyze her like this?

"Maybe it's time to think about what you want, Alex," Lu said quietly.

"What do you mean?"

"What do you want out of life? Because you may pretend living in this place you always wanted to get out of and running your dad's business is enough for you, but we know you better than that. Do you want to change your future? Do you want a relationship? A family?"

"And whatever future you imagine," Owen said, "do you think Bridget fits into it?"

"Or if she doesn't right now, could she?" Lu asked.

Alex scratched the wooden tabletop with her thumbnail. "Why are you guys ganging up on me all of a sudden?"

"We're not ganging up on you, sweetie," Jordan assured her. "It's just... when you and Bridget were at your best, you were at the top of the world."

"Yeah, and it was a really long way to fall."

"And you picked yourself up, came away stronger than you started. Maybe those obstacles that broke you before wouldn't break you now."

Alex shook her head. "What are you saying?"

"We just don't want you to give up on something just because you got hurt once."

"I could get hurt again," Alex murmured. Because that was it. That was the truth of things. What if she worked up enough courage to put the past behind her only for Bridget to leave again? She didn't think she could survive that.

In fact, she *knew* she couldn't.

Jordan reached over. "Look, we all make mistakes."

"Some of us make bigger mistakes than others," Lu said.

"The point is that you were happy with Bridget, and, while you're not exactly happy now, I think you can see a glimmer of it. I think you know what you want. We just don't want to see you give up on something wonderful because of mistakes made when you were twenty-three."

They were different people now. Who knew if they would even get along anymore? But they would, Alex realized with a sharp intake of breath. If you stripped away all the pain, all the guilt, they still got along wonderfully. And if that was something Alex could have again, if it was something within their reach, didn't she deserve a shot at it?

All this time she'd tried to convince herself she didn't love Bridget anymore, and all this time, she'd been lying to herself.

"And if it's not Bridget," Owen said, "then it'll be someone else. But we don't want to see you resign yourself to being alone when you deserve to be loved and to be happy."

"Yeah, let us set you up. Let us make you an online dating profile," Lu said.

The single life wasn't her first choice, but it worked for her. Or at least, it had.

"Do you think..." Alex swallowed hard past a lump in her throat. "Do you think it could ever work?"

Owen covered her hand with his own. "I think you won't know until you ask her."

Alex pulled it away to rub her face. "I can't. I can't do that."

"Okay, okay," Lu said, holding up her hands. "So, don't ask her outright."

"Then what am I supposed to do?"

"You ask her out."

"On a date?"

"Yes, genius, on a date," Lu said with an affectionate eye-roll. "Just be together for a few hours without any pressure, see if she still makes you laugh, if you still connect with her like you did before."

"It's a date, not a marriage proposal." Jordan beamed at her. "You can do it."

"Yeah, don't you think you owe it to yourself?" Owen asked.

Did she? Did she owe herself anything? At the very least, though, maybe she owed Bridget something. Something like a clean slate.

"We should definitely play 'She,'" Max said, "but do you think we should put 'Alexandra' on the set list?"

Bridget, lost in her own thoughts, listened to the question without really hearing it.

"Bridget?"

"Huh? What?" She swiveled on her stool to face him. "Sorry. What did you say?"

"I'm trying to finalize the set list, which is something you should have input in, I think."

"Yeah, that sounds good."

"You didn't even hear a word I said," Max said, no accusation in his voice. He tossed his notebook onto the table. "You can talk to me, you know."

"I know." And she usually did. He was the one who had nursed her through a broken heart, even if it was of her own making, and stood by her side during this whole journey. He was probably most responsible for keeping the fame from going to her head, and he was responsible for giving her the support she'd needed to come home.

"Well, you've been at this long enough not to freak out over a concert, so it must be something else."

She resituated herself so her legs were curled underneath her on the couch. "After the concert, we're leaving. I mean, obviously you don't have to come with me, but I want to leave." For some reason, admitting it out loud made her feel like a failure.

"Are you sure?" he asked softly.

"It's nice being with my family, but…"

There's nothing left for me here wasn't exactly right. There was lots to love about this town—her family, her friends, the weather, the way everyone was nice and no one seemed to want anything from her, the quiet.

"I can't take it anymore," she whispered.

Max took her hand and squeezed. "I understand. I'm ready to go back to New York when you are. We can be on a plane late Saturday night if that's what you want."

"Thank you. For being here and for everything. I don't know what I'd do without you."

"Probably get a lot fewer questions about us dating," he said.

She chuckled.

"Bridget!" The upstairs door creaked open and her mother shouted down, "There's someone here to see you."

"Oh, okay. Thanks."

That was weird. Usually, her mom said who it was or told her to come upstairs to greet her guest. But before Bridget could ask, the stairs creaked as the person descended.

When Alex came into view, Bridget vaulted off the couch.

"Um, hi," she said, surprised and pleased and nervous all at the same time. Her heart sped up at an unhealthy interval.

"Hi," Alex said. "Hi, Max."

"Hey." Max stood, too. "I'm going to go make some tea. I'll be back in a few minutes," he said. At the steps, he turned and gave Bridget a reassuring smile.

Bridget stuck her hands in the back pockets of her jeans just for something to do with them.

"Are these boxes from our old apartment?" Alex asked.

Bridget followed her gesture to the corner, where a handful of boxes labeled "A & B apt" resided. "Oh. Yeah, they are." She crossed the room. "You can look. If there's anything you want back..."

What was the protocol for this sort of thing? Should she offer to leave the room? Bridget herself hadn't touched the boxes out of fear she wouldn't be able to escape the memories.

Alex's gaze grew distant for a moment before she said, "That's not really why I came."

"Oh. Right." When Alex didn't say anything else, Bridget prompted, "So, why *did* you come? Not that I don't want you here, of course, or that you can't stop by. I just didn't really expect you. That's all." Great. Now she was rambling.

Alex seemed unfazed by it, though. In fact, she seemed in her own little world, hardly aware of Bridget at all. She wrung her hands, something she only did when she was extra nervous. She was normally so good at playing it cool, seemingly detached from all emotions. If Bridget's surprise return hadn't thrown her for a loop, what could be getting her this bent out of shape?

"Do you want to sit?" Bridget asked, sweeping a hand toward the futon. "Do you want a drink? Water? Coffee? Tea?"

Alex didn't even seem to hear the questions. Instead, she met Bridget's gaze and blurted, "Would you go on a date with me?"

Chapter Eleven

Then

FOR THE PAST MONTH, ALEX had spent every day, including weekends, at the café, meaning her schedule hadn't allowed for much free time. She and Bridget hadn't had a real conversation in at least a week, and as soon as she walked into the apartment on Sunday night, Alex could feel the tension. Benny rushed forward to greet her, but Bridget stayed on the couch, where she was watching old episodes of *Project Runway*.

Alex fixed herself a mug of tea before sitting down beside Bridget. "Did you eat dinner yet?"

Bridget nodded. "I went out with Jordan and Lu."

Unsure of what to say, Alex sipped her tea. They'd been together for five years and friends for much longer. They'd experienced silence loads of times—when they were tired, when they were contemplative, when they just needed the quiet. It had never felt like this, so awkward, and Alex couldn't help but think it was all her fault.

Bridget leaned forward, picked up the remote from the coffee table, and muted the TV. Then she shifted to face Alex. "We should talk."

Uh-oh. The three worst words that could ever be uttered in a relationship. Alex kept sipping her tea. It wasn't that she shut down, exactly, but she was learning it was easier to get through these moments when she didn't fight them.

Bridget grasped Alex's forearm, shifting her thumb back and forth. "I miss you," she said softly. "Before, it was bad enough when work ran you ragged, but I could deal with it. Now, you spend all your time at a café you said you had every intention of selling."

Alex stayed quiet.

"You *are* going to sell it, right?" Bridget asked.

Alex tightened her jaw and stared into her tea. The café was the last thing she had left of her dad. She *had* had every intention of selling it. Then she'd stepped inside and found she couldn't let go of the memories they'd made there. "I said I'd think about it."

"And that's fine, Lex. Don't sell it if you really don't want to. You know I'll support you in whatever you do, but, babe..." Bridget paused. "This isn't a life, and we can't go on like this."

"So it's my fault." Alex's voice was flat. That was who she was now, someone who sleepwalked through her days.

Bridget scooted closer. "Alex, no, that's not what I said."

Alex focused on her breathing. This was just a rough patch. She wouldn't always feel this way, and when she felt better, Bridget would feel better too. They could be happy again. They would.

Bridget shrugged with one shoulder. "I don't know. I don't know what the answer is. But maybe we need to explore what we want. Separately."

Alex finally looked up into Bridget's clear eyes. "What are you saying?"

Bridget licked her lips. "I'm saying I want to go to New York for a little while. I'm serious about my music career, and that's the next logical step for me. I've got a friend there. Max. I've talked about him. He knows some people, says he can get us a few gigs, maybe get our stuff heard by the right crowd."

Alex set down her tea and put her head in her hands. She'd never survive a separation, not now. When she finally spoke, the words came out low and hoarse. "I need you."

"Do you? Because you don't let me hold you or talk to you or comfort you." Bridget's voice wasn't cruel, just sad. "And what about what I need? We barely see each other, and when we do, we barely talk." She swiped a hand through her hair. "Can we even call this a relationship?"

Fuck. Alex knew something would break eventually. She just didn't expect it to be *them*. They were solid. Even if her dad's death had rocked their foundation a little, they were solid.

Bridget came even closer, rubbed the back of Alex's neck. "Look, baby, I know things have been hard for you, but I really think we could use a break. We just keep putting pressure on ourselves. If we don't do something about it, we'll implode." She rested her forehead against the side of Alex's head. "Why not try the long distance thing for a while? I'll go to New York for a few months and play some shows and network. You can stay here, or move back home, and decide how the café fits into our future."

Sighing, Alex scrubbed her face. She didn't want to stay without Bridget, but she didn't want to go to New York, either. She didn't know what she wanted.

"And there won't be any pressure. No timeline," Bridget continued. "Just us making informed decisions about what we want."

Alex let out a long, shuddering breath. Bridget deserved more than her. Bridget had big dreams, and she'd never be satisfied with less. Maybe Alex should just give up now.

But she couldn't. She was selfish. She couldn't let go of the only woman she'd ever loved. She twisted into Bridget's embrace, buried her face in the curve of her neck.

Bridget's arms came around her. "What do you need, baby?" she murmured. "Please tell me what you need."

"You," Alex whispered, and then she kissed Bridget, and there was no more talking that night.

Now

Alex was in the process of stripping out of her fourth choice of flannel shirt when her doorbell rang. Cursing, she ran a hand through her hair and dashed down the steps, Benny at her heels.

Lu and Owen were at the door, Owen carrying Keiko in that little backpack thing she seemed to love.

Alex squeezed Keiko's chubby cheeks and dropped a kiss on her forehead. "Thank God you guys are here."

"You don't have to pretend," Owen said. "I know I only got invited because I literally bring the cuteness."

Rolling her eyes, Alex led them up to her room, where clothes littered her bed, the chair in the corner, and the floor.

"Holy hell," Lu said, laughing.

Owen covered Keiko's ears. "Watch it, please."

"She doesn't understand it."

"She will someday."

Lu's eyeroll was surprisingly fond. "Fine. I will attempt to curb my sailor's mouth."

Alex mustered up a glare. "Did you come to help or not?"

"Okay, calm down." Lu rummaged through the closet. "First of all, you've got good instincts going with a flannel because that girl loves you in flannel."

Alex's cheeks burned. "She does?"

"Oh, yeah," said Owen. "Ever wonder why Lu hid all your flannels that one summer?"

Heh, she'd forgotten about that. "I wondered why they mysteriously reappeared in my closet right around the time I was packing to go back to school."

"I had to stop you two from being unbearably cute somehow." Lu tossed a pair of black jeans at her. "Take those off. Put these on. They make your butt look better."

"Oh, um…" Should that even be an issue today? Maybe she should look casual, like they were just old friends going for coffee.

Except she knew with certainty now that wasn't what she wanted

She stripped out of her cargo pants and stepped into the jeans. Next, Owen chose a forest-green T-shirt bearing her bar's logo. Lu picked out a blue-and-green flannel to match.

"And…" The last piece Owen handed her was a light quilted vest.

She threw it on and held out her arms. "How do I look?"

"Very gay," Lu said.

Giggling, Keiko wiggled her arms. Alex took that as approval.

Bridget fixed her hair in the living room mirror above the mantel. She'd never felt so nervous and so calm at the same time. Nervous because Alex might want her back—at least wanted a date. Calm because that was what love did.

And it *was* love. She'd never stopped being in love with Alex.

Which meant today could be the start of their second chance. She blew out her breath in a measured whoosh, turning to face Max on the couch. "Do I look okay?"

"You look amazing," he said. "How are you feeling?"

"A little nauseated, a little thrilled."

He lifted a knowing eyebrow. "You've dated one of the biggest movie stars in the country."

"This is different."

"I know. I'm just saying to breathe and be yourself. She loved you once. She'll love you again."

Bridget hoped so. Before she could lose her nerve, the doorbell rang.

Max threw one arm around her shoulders and squeezed. "Go. Have a great time. I'll be here when you get back."

"Thanks." She kissed him on the cheek. He was the best friend she could ask for. Even now, when she should be concentrating on the concert, he wasn't on her back to practice. He wasn't yelling about distractions. Instead he was telling her to put herself first, encouraging her to go on this date. She'd spent so long putting her career first, pushing everything else down, that it had no place to go but right back up.

Between the living room and the foyer, Bridget managed to convince herself this was all an elaborate hoax. It wouldn't be Alex at the door. It would be Lu or Owen or Jordan or Riley, telling her to move on and get a life.

But it wasn't a hoax. Alex stood on the porch, looking sexy as hell in a flannel and vest.

Breathe, Bridget, she told herself. *Just breathe.*

"Hi," Alex said shyly.

"Hi."

Alex stuffed her hands into her pockets. "So, uh, are you ready to go?"

"Oh, yeah, of course." Bridget willed herself to calm down as she pulled the door shut behind her and followed Alex to the truck.

"Where are we going?" she asked as Alex held the passenger door open. Alex didn't reply until she slid into the driver's seat. "You'll see."

"You're really not going to tell me?"

"I'm really not going to tell you."

"That's not fair," Bridget said, laughing. But she turned her attention to the radio, settling on the only station in town that played popular music—and regretting that decision when the current song ended and one of hers came on. She reached for the dial. "Sorry. I'll—"

"It's okay," Alex said. "I like this song."

She did? She'd *heard* this song? Her mom had said that Alex never picked up the CDs Bridget had sent for her, and Lu had given her the impression that Alex switched off the radio or TV anytime Bridget came on.

Before she could contemplate this shift in attitude, Alex said, "I have two conditions for today."

Conditions? Bridget's heart lurched in her ribcage. She'd thought this was a date, not a negotiation. "Okay..."

"The first is that we don't talk about the past."

Bridget smiled. She'd readily agree to that, especially if it meant no more trying to figure out who shared more of the blame. "I can do that. And the second?"

"We don't talk about the future."

"There's only today?"

"That's right."

The truth was, Bridget burned to talk about the future. What did this date mean? What did she even *want* it to mean? She could push that down, though. She could be present in the here and now and worry about the future in the morning. "Okay," she agreed.

"Okay," Alex said, "and thank you."

Bridget didn't say anything because she knew Alex, knew it meant Alex didn't know exactly how she felt yet. She wanted today to be today and nothing else, and maybe, tomorrow, it could be something more. But Alex always hedged her bets, always made her decisions around the possibility of getting hurt.

And after all this time, the thing they agreed on most was that they didn't want to hurt each other—or get hurt by each other—again.

So, she relaxed. There was only today, and she intended to have fun and make the most of it.

It wasn't long before Alex pulled into the parking lot of Sunberry Farms. Bridget couldn't contain her grin. They used to come here every summer to pick strawberries and every fall to pick apples and pumpkins. She had so many good memories associated with this place, and she was touched that Alex thought of it.

"You could've told me," Bridget said as she hopped out of the truck.

Alex walked around the front of the vehicle to join her and shrugged. "I wanted it to be a surprise. But you're okay with it, right?"

"Of course I am."

"Good. Ready?"

Bridget inhaled the fresh scents of hay and apples and fall. There was nothing like a warm day out in the October sunshine walking beside the woman you adored. And since there was no yesterday, no tomorrow, only today, Bridget decided to be bold and reach for Alex's hand.

Alex didn't pull it back.

They started their trip at the market, an outdoor area with wooden booths featuring crafters, florists, small brewers, and more. Once upon a time, they used to take turns buying each other flowers. Neither of them made a move today, though. Instead, they bought cups of cider to sip as they strolled.

Past the market was the kids' activity area and the ticket booths. They got two tickets for the hayride, the only way to get to the orchard. It rolled by every fifteen minutes, and, as the next was still at least five minutes away, they chatted about nothing, falling into a familiarity that threatened Bridget's promise not to think about the future.

When the tractor pulling the hayride rattled up, Alex helped her onto it. She chose the hay bales in the back corner and took delight in the way Alex sat close enough that their thighs pressed together.

"Are you thinking what I'm thinking?" she asked.

Alex rolled her eyes. "About that time we rode the haunted hayride during their fright nights?"

"Uh-huh."

"I know what you're going to say."

"You were so scared."

"I...was. I definitely was," Alex said, joining in Bridget's laughter. "I hate people jumping out at me. I don't understand why people like that."

"It's an adrenaline rush."

"There are way better adrenaline rushes out there."

"We were stupid in high school."

"Yeah, we were."

Alex's eyes were shining brightly. Bridget bit her lip as she admired the view.

"We came back every year," Alex said in a more sober voice, "and even though everyone wanted to go on the haunted hayride, you always stayed behind with me."

Bridget bumped her shoulder. "Yeah, well, being with you was way better than any silly ride."

"Mm."

When they reached their destination, as they dismounted, a farm employee handed them a bushel basket to share. The orchard was gorgeous, fragrant, and full of light. Little kids shouted and screamed as they ran around their parents' legs and through the rows of trees.

While Bridget preferred honeycrisp, Alex favored ginger gold, and they had long since learned how to go about the picking in a methodical manner. They started in the honeycrisp section.

Though they'd done this more than once, it'd been a while for Bridget, and she was out of practice. She no longer had a good sense for what height she could reach. By the time Alex had gathered four, she still had none.

"You know you could get the ones closer to the ground with far less effort," Alex said, chuckling.

"They don't taste as good," Bridget said.

"Pretty sure they taste the same." Alex set their basket on the ground. "Need some help?"

"What, you think you can reach the high ones?"

"No. I think we can do it together."

And then Alex was turning her back to Bridget and leaning down and waiting.

"We're not teenagers anymore, Lex," said Bridget. "What if I hurt you?"

"You won't. I promise," Alex said over her shoulder. She flicked a smile Bridget's way. "Besides, we've got to get you those high apples."

Shaking her head, Bridget said, "If you're sure," and hopped onto Alex's back. She hooked her legs around Alex's waist. If things like this kept happening, she wasn't going to be able to keep her promise not to think about the past, either.

But they'd already broken that one anyway, hadn't they? And since that was the case, maybe Alex would let them keep breaking the rules.

"Come on, Bridge. Reach!" Alex said.

Bridget did, and her fingers closed around a deliciously ripe apple.

"So…" Bridget said.

Alex tapped her fingers against the steering wheel as they pulled away from the farm. It used to be there would be no question that the date would continue. They'd hang out at the diner or the library or one of their parents' houses. Now, Bridget was fishing for an answer to the question they never used to need to ask.

"Well," Alex said, "I know it's kind of silly, but I was thinking we could take the apples back to my place and make a pie. And while it's baking, I could cook us dinner."

"That's not silly. That sounds great."

"Good." Alex's breath hitched in her throat. She'd been worried about planning this date. After all, Bridget was a big-city girl now. What if her fame had changed her and she expected something fancier than this?

But in fact, the whole afternoon had been lovely. The problem was, Alex couldn't seem to stop waiting for the other shoe to drop. This was what she did. She got in her own head and couldn't let herself enjoy anything.

She forced that train of thought to a screeching halt. To take her mind off it, she used a technique Lu had taught her shortly after the breakup. She tapped into her senses in order to drop into the present moment and not dwell on what could be. Bridget had turned the radio to the '90s channel, and the song drifting out of the speakers was something upbeat by a boy band she'd never cared for. She felt the smooth vinyl of the steering wheel against her hands.

She chanced a glance at Bridget, who was humming under her breath and bopping her head to the music, and she calmed.

Until she pulled into her own driveway, that was.

The last time Bridget had stepped foot inside the house, it had still belonged to Alex's dad. What would she think of the things Alex had changed? The things she hadn't changed?

Benny greeted them with kisses as they walked through the front door, and Bridget sank to her haunches to pet him. "Hey, buddy. How you doing? I miss you, too. I miss you so much."

Alex deposited the bushel of apples on the kitchen island. She was opening two bottles of beer when Bridget padded into the kitchen, Benny on her heels.

Bridget gulped hers as soon as Alex handed it to her. "You know I haven't baked in forever, right? I'm going to be terrible at this."

"It's a pie, not rocket science," Alex said. "You skin the apples and cut them up."

For someone who appeared so confident, and had ample reason to be so, Bridget doubted herself a lot. Was it bad that Alex hoped it was because of her? Hoped that she, a small-town girl with not a lot going for her, could knock a Grammy Award winner off her game? Just a little bit?

"But the crust," Bridget said. "Beyond me. My grandma is so disappointed."

Alex chuckled, picturing Grandma Callahan's stern face. "That's why the person who's not going to substitute salt for sugar is on crust duty."

"No promises, but I'll do my best to cut these apples in a way that would make Granny proud. Aprons?"

"Middle drawer over there, but I'm not wearing one."

"Oh, yeah? Why not? Bridget grabbed two aprons from the drawer and tied one around herself.

"I'm not scared of flour like someone is," Alex murmured, a satisfied smirk on her lips.

Bridget's mouth dropped open. She snatched a towel hanging on the oven and swatted Alex's shoulder. "We were seven! You knew I was afraid of ghosts!"

Alex bit her bottom lip as she laughed. "Okay, okay. I'll wear the apron on as my penance. How's that?"

"I'm satisfied."

"Good. Can we please make a pie now?"

In response, Bridget set about washing the apples and placing them on a cutting board.

Alex retrieved ingredients for the crust, glancing at Bridget while trying not to be too obvious about it.

Bridget watched while trying to make it seem like she wasn't. She was captivated by the way Alex's T-shirt rode up when she reached for a bowl, the way the muscles in her forearm jumped as she mixed the dough.

Alex had both changed and not changed in the five years they'd been apart. Her features had matured, and she'd put muscle on her frame, but the way she moved was as familiar to Bridget as if they'd shared an apartment only yesterday.

Bridget licked her lips, which were suddenly dry.

They worked in a comfortable quiet until she finished washing the apples, took out her phone, and turned on some music.

As Bridget cut up the first apple, Alex said, "You should put them in water so they don't brown while you're cutting the rest."

"Right." Bridget slid around Alex to reach into the top cabinet above the dishwasher. She pulled out a bowl and filled it partway with water. It was only when she brought it to the island that she realized Alex was staring. "What?"

Blinking, Alex looked away. She kneaded her knuckles into the dough. "Nothing. It's just... I left everything where it was. I guess I shouldn't be surprised."

"I haven't forgotten anything," Bridget said quietly. "About this town, about this house."

About you, she wanted to say, but feared Alex wouldn't take it well.

Alex cleared her throat and placed half the dough on the island to roll out.

Once the pie was in the oven, Alex ushered Bridget onto a stool at the island and served her another beer. Instead of getting another herself, she poured a glass of water. Better not to let herself get too loose.

"You're really not going to let me help?" Bridget asked.

"We don't want a repeat of Thanksgiving, do we?"

Bridget hung her head in her hands, but her shoulders shook with laughter. "I'm never going to live that down, am I?"

"Considering it was the first holiday we hosted in our apartment and it ended in getting pizza delivered, I'm going to say nope."

"I swear I'm a little bit better than that now."

"A little bit? Way to inspire confidence."

"Fine," Bridget said with a perfect eye roll. "I admit you're right—probably—to keep me out of dinner preparations."

Alex swept a bow. "Thank you. And with that, I'll get on with it."

As she took out ingredients for chicken parmesan, she held her breath, waiting for Bridget to comment. Because it was Bridget's favorite dish.

Bridget, thankfully, didn't comment. Instead, she said, "So, tell me about the bar."

Alex put water on the stove to boil and measured out the spaghetti. "What about the bar?"

Bridget shrugged. "Why'd you decide to open it?"

"Well, I liked being in the café. When I was there, I liked that it still felt like my dad was with me. So after a year went by, and I realized I probably wasn't going to sell, probably wasn't going to move, I started thinking about how I could make it my own. When the bar next door went up for sale, I bought it with the life insurance money." She shrugged. "I just wanted to leave my mark."

Bridget smiled. "You've certainly done that. I hear nothing but rave reviews."

"Thanks." Alex brushed her hands on her apron. Not that she needed Bridget's approval.

"And the brewery?"

"Well, when you own a bar and want to expand... It seemed like a natural step."

"Are you using your degree at all?" Bridget asked, a hint of wistfulness in her voice.

Alex paused as she shredded the cheese. She cleared her throat. "Not really."

"Do you miss it?"

Did she? She missed being conversational in more than just English, missed the way she used to seek out movies and books in other languages. Nowadays, when she wasn't working, she was usually too tired to tax her brain with foreign languages. And she always had wanted to travel. "I miss

139

aspects, I guess. My life's turned out differently than I thought it would, but…not badly. I'm okay with the direction it's taken."

"Good," Bridget said. "I'm glad."

And Alex smiled because although she didn't need Bridget's approval, she liked it all the same.

Bridget leaned back in her chair, hands on her full and very happy belly. "That was incredible. I had no idea you could cook *that* well."

Alex shrugged. "Maybe you're just so used to your own cooking that anything more than microwavable meals tastes exceptional."

"Are you ever going to stop teasing me about my cooking skills?"

"Or lack thereof? No, I don't think so."

That was fine with Bridget, especially if the 'ever' implied what she hadn't meant to imply at all.

Alex set her napkin on the table next to her plate. "Well, are you ready for the pie?"

"Of course!" Bridget followed Alex into the kitchen, taking out her phone as she went. As Alex held a knife over it, she said, "Wait! I want to get a picture of this."

"What? Why?"

"Because we made a pie together! How exciting is that?" Bridget snapped a few photos in quick succession.

"Are you going to post it?" Alex asked as she cut into the pie. "Your followers would go crazy."

"Can I?" Bridget asked, self-conscious. Alex didn't love social media, and Bridget didn't want to give the impression she was using Alex for likes or to boost her image.

"Sure." Alex cut two pieces, plated them, and added a dollop of vanilla ice cream to each.

Bridget cropped one of the photos so Alex's face wasn't visible, just her arms and part of her flannel. She tapped her thumbs against the phone case. "How should I caption it?" Usually, she went for upbeat and grateful, but she didn't want to seem too sappy, and she definitely didn't want to write anything Alex would regret—even if no one but their closest friends and family would know she was the person in the picture.

She wrote: *Thanks to Sunberry Farms for the apple-picking experience! I've never been known for my skills in the kitchen, but I can't wait to taste this pie.*

She had her account set so that the only notifications she would get were from the few people she followed, like friends and family. Still, she switched her phone to silent mode and set it on the island before picking up her plate and following Alex into the living room. No distractions

Benny trotted behind them and settled himself at their feet. Alex fed him a piece of crust.

"Delicious," Bridget said a few minutes later as she put her empty plate on the coffee table.

"We make a pretty good team," Alex said quietly.

"We do," Bridget agreed.

They were close now, close enough that Bridget's body instinctively responded to the proximity. Her breath came sharp and deep, and her heart thudded fast. There was nothing she wanted more in this moment than to kiss Alex.

A thousand thoughts rushed through her mind. Would Alex push her away? Did Alex want it, too? This *was* a date, so a kiss wouldn't be entirely unexpected, would it?

She leaned forward, the movement slow and subtle. And then she held her breath and waited.

Alex's gaze drifted between Bridget's eyes and lips and then back again. Bridget's pupils were blown, the desire clear, as were her intentions. Yet she stayed where she was, mere inches away.

It was Alex's choice to pull away or not.

Alex's choice to move forward or keep running from their past.

There's only today.

Shouldn't they make the most of it?

Alex slid her palm to Bridget's cheek. Bridget closed her eyes and sighed like she'd come home. Maybe she had. Maybe they both had.

Alex didn't need to think about the past. She didn't need to think about the future, either. All she needed was here and now. She could worry about the rest later.

For once, she stopped thinking and just started *feeling*. Felt Bridget's lips against hers. Felt Bridget's fingertips skating across her cheeks, her neck, curling into her hair. Felt the press of Bridget's curves against her body.

Felt the seed of ache in her heart blossoming into something tender and gentle and perfect.

Chapter Twelve

Then

THE CHATTER OF THE BAR provided a pleasant soundtrack as Bridget packed up her guitar and keyboard. The show had gone well enough, and she'd tried out a couple new songs that had been well received. Or as well received as they could be when she was just a local singer, and the bar patrons were more interested in their drinks than the background music.

Except for her friends. Lu, Jordan, and Owen were there to support her. The person she wanted there the most, though, was a no-show.

"Hey!" Lu's voice was bright as she approached the small corner stage. "What can I do to help?"

Bridget wiped her sweaty bangs off her forehead and shook her head. "No, that's okay." She was particular enough about her equipment that she liked to do everything herself.

"I'll get you a drink, then."

"I think I'm going to head home once I get all this packed up, actually."

"Oh. Are you sure?"

"Yeah, I'm just tired," Bridget said as she rolled up a cord.

"Do you need a ride?"

Before she could answer, the opening of the door caught her eye, and she froze.

Alex.

Bridget cleared her throat and continued wrapping the cord. The sight of her girlfriend used to send her heart soaring. Now, frustration overrode any happiness it sparked. They were just going through a rough patch. It wouldn't—couldn't—last forever.

Right?

By the time Alex had greeted their friends and exchanged polite small talk, Bridget had finished up.

"Ready?" Alex asked.

Bridget nodded. She bid her friends good-bye, and Alex helped her carry her equipment out to the car. The late summer night was hot, and once she hopped into the passenger's seat, she cranked up the air conditioning, leaned her head back, and closed her eyes.

"Tired?" Alex asked.

"Mm-hmm." She'd had the early shift at the coffee shop today and had another tomorrow. Maybe one day, her passion would pay off. Right now, the only thing it was doing was exhausting her.

She breathed deeply and let the car's rumble relax her.

A few minutes later, over the hum of the engine, Alex asked, "Are you mad I missed the show?"

Bridget opened her eyes. "I'm not mad. I'm upset. There's a difference."

Alex's jaw jumped, and her hands tightened on the wheel. After a long beat, she said, "You've played lots of shows. I've been to ninety-nine percent of them. I don't see why this one is an issue."

Bridget's first instinct was to scoff. Alex was so wrapped up in her own grief that she barely saw Bridget at all anymore.

Bridget didn't scoff, though. She couldn't. Her throat was too tight and her eyes were burning. She swallowed it down. "I know you've been busy, Alex. I know you've been…" Sad and devastated and all those messy emotions that accompanied a parent's death that were different for everyone.

When her dad had died, Bridget had *needed* Alex. She'd needed her best friend, and her best friend had been there for her—through long days when Bridget couldn't find any words at all, through long nights when Alex's sturdy embrace was the only thing that could calm Bridget. Alex had been there for Bridget, so why couldn't she let Bridget be there for her?

"I wrote a song for your dad," Bridget said. She'd saved it for last, had hoped Alex would be there by that point. "I know you miss him. I do, too. And I've tried to be patient, but you can't just keep shutting me out."

"I'm not shutting you out. I need to be at the café."

"All day every day? You said your schedule would get easier. You said you'd make time for me."

"It's complicated, Bridget." Even in the dark, even in profile, Alex's frown was visible.

"Then tell me." Bridget reached over to put her hand on Alex's thigh. "That's why I'm here."

"It's all I've got left," Alex said softly.

Bridget squeezed gently. "That's not true. I've been trying to tell you that."

Alex didn't respond as she pulled into the parking lot of their building. As they climbed out and approached the door, she said, "Can we just drop it for the night?"

"Sure."

After all, that was what they always did.

When Bridget had put away her equipment, showered, and changed into soft pajamas, she slid into bed and pulled the covers up. Alex wasn't in bed yet. She was probably still in the living room, on her laptop, going over the books for the café and weighing renovation plans against potential price points and all the businessy things Bridget didn't care for.

So Bridget closed her eyes.

Later, in the middle of the night, when Alex finally came to bed, Bridget stirred awake. She curled into her girlfriend, grateful for the warmth but also craving her presence. The truth was she *missed* Alex. As much as it was possible to miss a person who was in the same room, a person who was supposed to her everything.

Alex, instead of reciprocating the embrace, turned away. And Bridget couldn't hide from the truth any longer. Sooner or later, something had to give.

Now

Alex woke slowly, coming to with a deep breath but refusing to open her eyes. It was warm. The sun shone through the window and right onto the bed, warming the sheets, warming her skin. Her muscles were pleasantly sore. She was usually an early riser, but she could sleep for another few hours without complaint.

There were better things to be doing, though.

She reached over to the other side of the bed only to grasp at air and sheets. Finally opening her eyes, she sat up. The bathroom door was cracked open, and through it, Bridget's bare back was visible.

Then Bridget's voice, low, trying not to wake her. "Pip, why do you need to know this now? Why do we need to talk about when I'm coming back to New York when I have a concert to play and an album to write?"

A pause.

"Sunday? God, Pip, that's… That's soon."

The conversation continued, but Alex stopped listening. It wasn't really her place. Besides, she'd heard all she needed to. She'd heard enough to remind her of the reality of their situation.

Bridget had a career back in New York. She had a *home* there. She didn't belong in a place this small, this static and stationary. She needed vibrancy, excitement. She needed a city as energetic as she was.

And that meant this couldn't work. Because Alex couldn't go to New York. She had friends here. She had a career here, and it was so much more than just taking care of her father's business now. She couldn't drop that to follow Bridget to a different state.

Tears burned, but she refused to let them fall. Not yet. As quietly as she could, she scooped up her jeans and bra and grabbed a fresh T-shirt and underwear from a drawer. She tiptoed down the stairs and dressed in the living room, using the physical movement to keep her mind off the sadness that threatened to spill out of her like a tsunami.

After filling Benny's food bowl and topping up his water bowl, she filled the coffee machine and leaned on the counter to wait as it brewed. She'd had vague thoughts of making Bridget breakfast, but that had been when she'd only been thinking about the now. They both had futures to consider, and how could they make such diverse ones fit together?

And as much as that made her want to run in order to protect her heart, she couldn't do that. Not again. She wasn't twenty-three anymore, terrified out of her mind by things beyond her control. She was an adult, and she was going to prove it.

No matter how much it hurt.

The coffee machine beeped. She poured two mugs and carried them upstairs, Benny clomping after her.

Bridget ended the call with Pippa and let out a frustrated sigh. She wanted to throw her phone out the window. Or toss it in the shower and turn on the spray.

Instead, she splashed cool water on her face, braced her hands on the sink, and regarded her reflection absently. She'd been laser-focused her entire career. She could afford a night off, even if it was two days before a big charity concert. Why didn't Pippa see that when she was happy, she made better music?

And Alex made her happy.

The thought of Alex brought a grin to Bridget's face. Time to get back to that woman. She could have another hour—or maybe five—of basking in this happiness.

Careful not to let the door squeak, she shuffled out of the bathroom and into Alex's adjoining bedroom.

Only to find an empty bed, the sheets mussed and twisted. Shit. Alex must have woken up. The clock on the nightstand read a little after seven. Maybe she was making breakfast. She always did make the best pancakes.

Bridget slipped into her underwear and rummaged in Alex's T-shirt drawer until she found an oversized one. She was just running her fingers through her tangled hair in an attempt to tame it when Alex, dressed and carrying two mugs of steaming coffee, walked back in. She set one on the side table nearest Bridget, climbed back into bed, and chuckled as Benny jumped up and settled between her legs.

Bridget's heart warmed at the sight. Alex hadn't run away. That had to be a good sign. Bridget perched next to her on the bed, legs crossed.

"Hey," she said softly.

"Hey," Alex replied.

Bridget picked up her coffee, sipped, and let out a contented sigh. Alex had remembered just how she liked it. "Did I wake you?"

Alex nodded.

"Shit. I'm sorry."

"It's fine. That was Pippa on the phone?"

"Yeah." Bridget frowned at the reminder. Pippa might know what was best for her career, but Bridget knew what was best for herself. What if the two no longer lined up?

"Today's turned into tomorrow," Alex said softly, staring into her mug.

Bridget's heart dropped. That was what they'd agreed to—one day. One day that had bled into one night. It was morning now, though, and things looked different in the cold light of day. "What are you saying?"

"Your life isn't here, Bridget. You know it's not." She said it without malice or hurt, just stating a fact.

What if it could be? Her heart was split in two—Alex on the one side and music on the other. What did she have to do to stitch those halves together?

Eyes watering, Bridget put down her coffee. "You're saying you don't want to give us a shot? That's it? We're done, just like that?"

Alex set down her own coffee and gently nudged Benny to the bottom of the bed so she could face Bridget. "All I'm saying is, maybe the timing's just not right. Maybe we need to think about what we want and whether we can have our careers and each other."

After taking a deep breath to center herself, Bridget crawled onto Alex's lap and wrapped her arms around Alex's neck. The proximity was intoxicating. For a moment, all she wanted to do was breathe in Alex's calming, woodsy scent.

"There's nothing I want more than you," she murmured.

Alex closed her eyes. "You say that now, but will you still think that in a month? In a year? Can someone like you really be with someone like me? We belong in two different worlds."

"Someone like you? Someone who's intelligent and kind and when she loves, loves fiercely? I'd be honored to be with someone like you."

"Bridget..."

Bridget rested her forehead on Alex's. "Why are you ending this before it has a chance to really begin?"

"I can't move to New York with you."

"I'm not asking you to."

"So, what? Long distance? I don't want to do that, either." Alex pulled away to brush Bridget's hair behind her ear. "I didn't really think this far ahead."

Bridget opened her mouth and closed it again. Alex didn't need to be persuaded to talk about it, to figure out the logistics of a relationship split between Pennsylvania and New York.

Bridget brushed her lips over Alex's forehead. "That's not what this is about, is it?"

Alex couldn't meet Bridget's gaze. Bridget kissed her, gently, two, three, then four times until Alex murmured, "Are you going to leave again? Am I going to be enough this time?"

"Oh, baby…" Bridget held her tight. "We're older now. We're mature enough to make it work."

Tears glistened in Alex's eyes. "I just… I don't know if I'm ready."

Bridget ran her thumbs over Alex's cheeks. "Okay. Okay, baby. We don't have to rush this. We don't have to decide this now."

Alex nodded and murmured, "Okay."

"We can talk after the concert."

"And before you leave for New York."

"Yeah. Before that." Bridget twined her fingers into Alex's hair, and she sank down into Alex's lap. In this moment, they were the only two people in existence. She intended to hold onto that. "Until then, do one thing for me?"

"What?"

"Kiss me."

Alex did.

After she and Bridget parted, the morning plodded on, and Alex moved through it in a daze. This was for the best. It had to be.

Was this how Bridget had felt when she'd left the first time?

Her phone buzzed repeatedly, but she didn't answer any of the texts, didn't even open most of them. They were all from Lu, Jordan, and Owen, their inquiries about the date slowly morphing into outright concern at her silence. But she couldn't face them.

Couldn't face the fact that the universe had handed them a second chance, and she was simply throwing it away. They couldn't be together, and she never should've gotten her hopes up that they could. They were from completely different worlds now, led completely different lives.

The likelihood that her friends would understand that was low, and she didn't want to have to explain it, not when it felt like every thought of Bridget only cut her heart open again.

So she hid. She hid in the back office of the bar and buried herself in the accounts, making sure everything was in order. It was. Everything was always in order because this bar and the brewery and the café next door were the only real things in her life. At the end of the day, they were the only things she had, and she didn't neglect them.

In the early afternoon, she had to stumble out for food. Once her burger and fries were up, she turned to head back to her office and got stopped by Owen.

"Hey," he said warmly. "You haven't been answering any of our texts, so I came to check on you."

"I have a lot of work to do," she said, moving to walk past him.

He stepped into her path. "Well, wait. How'd last night go?"

"I don't want to talk about it."

"Alex, don't do this. Don't shut me out."

"I said I don't want to talk about it," she said again, more firmly this time. Without waiting for his acquiescence, she brushed past him and into her office. She closed the door behind her, set the food on her desk, and sank into her chair.

She didn't drink on the job, but today might be the day she started.

Instead, though, she rested her arms on her thighs and leaned forward until her breathing slowed down.

This wasn't the end of the world. Her life had fallen apart before, and she'd put it back together. She could do that again.

Couldn't she?

Bridget Callahan had never done a walk of shame. She'd never needed to because her first major relationship had been Alex, followed by a period of singlehood, and then what she'd had with Patrick had been steady and unhurried. Even after her first single had hit the charts and she'd become a household name almost overnight, she'd never partied too hard or lost control. So, no, she'd never done a walk of shame.

Until now.

She could only hope no one would notice her walking down the street in yesterday's clothes and post about it online. At least they were sensible clothes, and she didn't have to toddle home in five-inch heels that were murder on her feet.

The one silver lining in all this.

As she walked through the front yard, through the kitchen window, she saw her mom bustling about. Thankfully, there was a separate entrance to the basement, which meant she could sneak upstairs and bypass the awkward questioning. Maybe she'd be able to pretend she got home late last night.

She was less physically exhausted than she was emotionally, but she still didn't go straight to bed. As loath as she was to wash last night away, it might be the only thing that kept her from shattering. So she stripped and tossed all her clothes in the hamper. Then she turned the shower to scalding and stepped in.

The hot water relaxed her muscles without relaxing her mind, which was stuck in a loop of memories—Alex in the sunshine at the farm; Alex across the dinner table; Alex in bed, lips swollen and hair tousled; and then, this morning, Alex sending her away. Over and over again the loop played. Over and over again her heart broke.

When Alex got something in her head, she didn't let it go easily. How the hell was Bridget supposed to convince her they could do this?

After thirty minutes, she forced herself out of the shower to towel off. She threw on sweatpants and an oversized sweatshirt before crawling under the covers. If she had any tears left, she'd still be crying. Because she didn't, and because she couldn't fall asleep like this, she turned on the TV for background noise and scrolled through old photos of her and Alex until her eyes got heavy.

Night had fallen by the time the door to Alex's office opened. She looked up as her three friends stepped inside and lined up in front of her desk.

"I'm busy," she said dismissively. She was quiet, sure, but she wasn't normally so outright mean, especially not to the few people who truly cared about her.

Lu pushed her rolling chair, with Alex still in it, to the other side of the desk, where Owen and Jordan were pulling three other chairs into the room to make a little circle.

"No. No, guys, I don't want to do this," Alex said, her voice bordering on whiny. "I just want to be left alone."

"We know, but this is an intervention," Jordan said.

"Yeah, you're not supposed to *want* to participate," Owen said.

"I don't need an intervention."

"I think you do," Lu said.

Jordan and Owen chimed in their agreement.

Sighing, Alex slumped in her chair. "Fine. Let's get it over with, then."

Jordan grabbed a paperweight shaped like a miniature dragon from Alex's desk. "This is the talking dragon, okay? Since I have it, I'll start. Alex, we love you so much, and we know you retreat into yourself when you're sad. It's exactly what happened before, when your dad died," she said gently, "and when Bridget left. We don't care if you're with Bridget or you're not or if you love her or you hate her. All we care about is you dealing with your emotions in a healthy way. We want you to talk to us, okay?"

She passed the dragon to Lu.

"Oh, um…" Lu said. "I kind of feel like that says it all, don't you? Just talk to us, Alex."

She set the paperweight in Alex's lap. Alex stared at it through watery eyes. Wasn't this exactly what Bridget had hated, too? Her tendency to shut down, to run away and not come back until she had successfully bottled up all her emotions?

And her friends were right. It wasn't healthy. She didn't want to be this person anymore. She didn't want to carry around so much hurt that she had to push it down in order to function.

She picked up the dragon and, holding it tightly in her palm, told her friends everything. She told them why Bridget left. She told them how she shared the blame. She told them about their date and how it had ended.

When she finished, Owen leaned forward and asked, "Why don't you think it can work?"

Alex shook her head. "We're not the same people we were."

"Of course not," Jordan said. "In fact, you're both smarter and more mature. I'd say you have a way better chance of making it last this time."

Alex's leg jiggled. She couldn't say it, couldn't give voice to the fear that threatened to consume her.

"Alex?" Jordan prompted.

Without taking her gaze from the dragon in her hands, Alex asked, "What if it doesn't last this time, either?"

There was the crux of it, the reason she found it so difficult to open herself up again, especially to someone who'd already hurt her.

Bridget wasn't that person anymore, though. She wasn't a twenty-three-year-old who thought running off was the best way to solve a problem. In fact, over the past few weeks, Bridget had shown amply that she'd changed, that she was sorry beyond words.

It was Alex who'd refused to forgive her, refused to forgive herself, really. Until this moment, she hadn't realized that she, too, needed to change. She'd started to let go of the anger, but she still had a lot of room to grow. She always would.

"You won't know until you try," said Lu.

"I don't know," Alex said.

"That's okay," Jordan said, rubbing Alex's knees. "You don't have to know right away. Just promise us you'll think about it?"

Alex nodded.

"Good," Owen said. "And when you need us, we'll be here every step of the way."

Bridget woke to a gentle hand on her shoulder.

Max sat on the edge of the bed. "Hey," he said. "I was getting worried about you."

"Wha' time'sit?" she asked, pushing into a sitting position.

"Almost one."

Shit. She'd slept all morning. The concert was *tomorrow*. She needed to be on top of her game, and right now, she was the furthest thing from. She rubbed her face. Her first instinct was to wallow. She wanted the comfort that came with wrapping a blanket around herself and burrowing into the couch and watching crappy reality television.

That wasn't what she needed, though. That wasn't what this town needed. They needed a concert that would bring in money so they could pay their teachers so their kids could have decent educations.

"Let me change into real clothes," she said as she headed to the bathroom to brush her teeth, "and then I'll be ready."

Max scrunched his face at her. "Are you sure?"

"Absolutely. We have a set list to finalize, three arrangements to finish, and I still can't get the second verse of 'In Another Universe' straight."

Max grinned. "I'll meet you downstairs."

Chapter Thirteen

Then

BRIDGET'S BAGS WERE PACKED, AND her decision was made. It was the right thing for them. It was the only thing for them. So why did she feel so fucking awful about it?

She zipped up her backpack and sat on the couch with Benny to wait for Alex. The rest of her bags were loaded in Ian's truck, and he'd already left for their mom's house. Her mom was being good enough to help her out by storing what she couldn't take and agreeing to pay her rent until she got on her feet. She'd already found a place with three other aspiring musicians. In her head, this had been in the works for weeks now. And Alex had never wanted to talk about it. So now, Bridget had to force the issue.

She felt sick.

When Alex finally came home, she walked through the door, stopped short at the sight of Bridget, and then stuffed her hands into her pockets. "What's going on?" she asked warily.

Standing, Bridget wiped her clammy palms on her jeans. Alex deserved the truth. She deserved for Bridget not to dance around the issue or mince words. So Bridget took a deep breath and said, "I'm moving to New York."

Alex's eyes began to water, but she swallowed hard, and no tears fell. That was Alex, burying everything until there was no room left in her chest.

Bridget stepped closer to put one hand on Alex's hip and slide the other against her cheek. "I owe it to myself to see where this could go, and I think you need time to heal that isn't compromised by me rushing you—even if I don't mean to."

And maybe Alex would see it as a wake-up call. She'd accept the translating job in DC that she'd told Bridget she hadn't gotten, the one Bridget now knew she'd lied about. DC could be a fresh start for her, something Bridget thought Alex desperately needed.

Alex still didn't say anything. She'd always been less quick with words than Bridget. She liked to process and weigh and take her time.

"It feels like I've been holding my breath," Bridget continued. "I want to live, Alex. I want you to live, too."

This decision was *because* she loved Alex, not despite it. But how to get Alex to understand that?

When Alex finally spoke, her voice was little more than a whisper. "You said you'd always take care of me."

Bridget remembered that promise. Of course she did. The first time, they'd been in Alex's freshman dorm room, and she'd made that promise countless times since. She rested her forehead against Alex's. "But I can't if you won't let me." Fuck, this was ripping her apart. And she couldn't even imagine what it was doing to Alex. "And this doesn't… This doesn't have to be good-bye."

"How can it not? You're going to a different state."

"One that's not far away. It's not the other side of the world, and it's the twenty-first century. We've got cellphones and Skype and e-mail."

Bridget couldn't stand it any longer, and she took advantage of Alex's silence to kiss her—*really* kiss her, like she'd never have another opportunity to memorize those soft lips, to breathe in Alex's calming scent. But she would, she would, she would. Once they did a little bit of soul-searching on their own, they'd have all the time in the world to be together.

"Everything's taken care of. You don't have to worry about a thing," Bridget said as she broke the kiss. "My mom's going to pay my half of the rent for the next two months until the lease is up. Then you can go home, be close to the café. So you don't have to worry about anything, not a thing. I promise, baby."

"Right. Right." Alex backed away a step. She could barely look at Bridget.

Bridget couldn't blame her. She grasped both of Alex's hands and squeezed. "I'll call you. I'll text you. This isn't the end. I swear to you."

Now

Bridget wasn't all that into exercise. Alex had always been the one to drag her to the gym or challenge her to a race. Before a concert, though, the best way she could calm her nerves was to go for a run. Not a fast one, because she wasn't fast. Not even a particularly long one. But she liked the ritual of it.

She dressed in warm leggings and a long-sleeved athletic jacket that covered her neck in preparation for the autumn chill. She tied her sneakers, cued up her running playlist, and hit the sidewalk. Each pound of her feet against the concrete tethered her to Earth. She wasn't a superstar making millions a year who got recognized on the streets and asked for autographs. She was just a woman with less-than-stellar athletic ability wheezing her way through a two-mile loop.

Music pounded in her ears, upbeat, almost frantic. She didn't try to keep time, just let the beat flow into her body like it was the source of her energy. Her mind went blank. It was only her right foot striking pavement followed by her left foot doing the same. It was only her lungs expanding and compressing. It was only the wind rushing past her face.

And if she was only these things, only the sum of them, then she couldn't be in pain.

Alex rubbed her hands together. She'd finished helping Riley set up the Marlow Brews booth and had a bit of time to kill before the festival officially opened.

"I'm going to take a walk around the park," she said.

Riley nodded and didn't question her.

Alex took a deep breath. She could do this. She could. With the festival springing up around her, she was more certain than ever that she and Bridget weren't meant to be. She was a small-town girl. She loved the quiet streets and the wide, open sky, and even the way everyone knew who she was. She didn't want to trade that in for anonymity, for being just another among millions.

It was a beautiful, sunny day, and the park was abuzz with activity. Town employees set up the stage for the concert, and the booths ringing the park were already getting great foot traffic even though the festival wasn't officially open yet.

She stepped off the path in the middle of the park to look around for Bridget but didn't see her. The concert wasn't for another few hours, which meant she was probably at home practicing and preparing.

This was stupid. When she turned around to leave, she knocked shoulders with someone, someone big and solid.

"Sorry," she said.

"Not a problem." This guy was definitely not a local, but he looked familiar somehow. He gave her a bright smile and held out his arms. "See? No damage done."

"Well, okay, then. Have a good day." Alex started to walk away.

"Wait."

She stopped. "Something I can help you with?"

"Yes, actually. Directions. To the Callahan house."

"Oh." She rubbed the back of her neck. She wasn't certain of much right now, but she did know she shouldn't be giving out the address of a famous musician to some random guy.

"Where are my manners?" He held out his hand. "I'm Patrick Norwood. She's my ex-girlfriend. I'm not a stalker or anything. Just here to support the concert. The problem is I wanted it to be a surprise, and she never actually told me where she lives…"

Right. Bridget's movie star ex-boyfriend.

Of fucking course.

She accepted the handshake. "Alex. I'll take you to her place."

"Really? That's awesome. Thanks." He shouldered his duffel bag and followed her to the truck.

The Callahan house was only a few minutes away by vehicle, and they were soon cruising down Main Street.

"Bridget was right," he said. "She always talked about how nice the people were."

"She talked about us?" Alex asked, surprised.

"All the time."

"Huh."

"This is so nice," he said as he studied the passing shops and houses. "Have you lived here long?"

"Born and raised."

"That's awesome."

Alex held back a snort of laughter. Only someone who didn't grow up in a tiny-ass town in the middle of nowhere would think that. She pulled up to the curb outside the Callahan house. "This is it."

"Thank you so much for the ride." Patrick said as he got out. Standing on the sidewalk with his bag shouldered, he took a hundred-dollar bill out of his wallet and held it out. "I really appreciate it."

Alex raised her eyebrows at the bill before shaking it off. "No problem."

"Are you sure? You took me out of your way."

"I'm sure."

"Well, thank you again," he said, putting the wallet back in his pocket and heading toward the house.

A crease formed in Alex's forehead. Part of her wanted to torture herself, wanted to stay and watch as Bridget opened the door and threw a hand over her mouth in surprise and pulled Patrick into an embrace.

But she was smarter than that. Or at least getting smarter. So before he reached the door, she shifted the truck into drive and pulled away. What Bridget did wasn't any of her business.

Not anymore.

Not ever.

"Patrick?" Bridget could hardly believe her eyes as she stepped into the living room, where Patrick jumped up from the couch to hug her. She considered him a friend, but beyond some catch-up and check-in texts, they hadn't spoken in-depth in weeks.

"It's so nice to see you, Bridget," he said.

She pulled back to look him in the eye. "How did you even get here?"

"Oh, my Lyft dropped me off at the park because that's where the concert is, but a local offered me a ride here. I had to explain I knew you, of course, and wasn't some obsessed fan."

The town was full of nice people and even more people who'd jump at the chance to drive a celebrity around their hometown.

"I think her name was Alex," he added.

Bridget's heart stuttered before it settled back into a normal rhythm. She curled her arms around herself. "Wh-what are you doing here?"

"It was Pippa's idea, actually. She thought if I introduced you at the concert, it would give you some good press," he said, his voice kind.

"Good, old Pippa," Bridget said, "always looking out for me. You came out of the breakup squeaky clean, though, so why agree to come all the way to small-town Pennsylvania for a weekend?"

"You know me. I can never resist the spotlight. Plus, I still care about you, Bridget, and I want to support you. If that's okay."

Bridget smiled. He always had been supportive of her music. "Of course it's okay. Thank you for coming."

He nodded and clapped his hands together. "Now, tell me what I can do."

He was no musician, but his famous mug would still give the concert a boost. Oh, her fans would love that. The gossip rags might take his sudden appearance the wrong way, though. Was that something she wanted to risk? Now, when things with Alex were so fragile?

Patrick nudged her shoulder. "I'm here if you just want to talk, too."

She looked straight into his clear blue eyes, saw honesty there.

He drew her to the couch, and they sat down facing each other. "If this has anything to do with what we talked about that night, I'm okay, Bridget. I promise. I'd like to think we're friends."

That night, the night they'd broken their engagement and she'd confessed that she'd never truly been able to move on from her last relationship. And Patrick, gentleman that he was, had understood.

Her lips twitched in a small, appreciative smile. "She..." That was all she managed before the tears burned her eyes and she knew she couldn't say anymore without letting them go. She swiped a finger under her eye.

"Have you seen her?" Patrick asked.

She nodded.

"Talked to her?"

More than that, even. So much more.

He read her silence. "You've only been here, what, a few weeks? Things like this—big things, the things worth doing—take time."

"That's what I said," Max called from the kitchen.

Bridget chuckled wetly, but she smiled when her best friend joined them in the living room with a cup of coffee for each of them. She took her mug gratefully and sipped down the lump in her throat. She cradled it against her chest, feeling the warmth spread into her palms. "She doesn't see a future for us," she said. "She thinks we're from two different worlds and that if we start something, we'll only end up breaking each other's hearts again."

Patrick and Max, both quiet, exchanged a loaded look.

"Well," Max said, sipping his coffee, "the only thing to do is change her mind."

"Gee, thanks for that insight," Bridget said. They didn't know Alex like she did. They didn't know how stubborn she could be. "How, exactly, do you suggest I do that?"

Patrick smiled charmingly. "Oh, a hometown sweetheart playing a charity concert that'll be broadcast all over the internet? I'm sure we can think of something."

"Did you guys hear that Patrick Norwood is going to introduce Bridget?" someone said as they walked by the Marlow Brews booth.

Alex, folding up the banner that hung on the front of the booth, suddenly found it hard to swallow. So, he wasn't just here for support. He was *involved* now. She placed the folded banner in a crate. It was none of her business anyway.

"You're not staying for the concert?" Riley asked, leaning against the booth's frame.

Alex indicated the crates loaded with their supplies, including the money pouch. "Someone's got to take this back to the bar."

"I can do it," Riley offered.

"That's okay. I've got to relieve Hunter anyway. He wants to come to the concert."

"Why don't you just close the bar?" Riley asked. "It's not like there will be anyone there anyway. They'll all be here."

Alex shrugged. "We've never closed during the festival any other year."

"Yeah, and Bridget Callahan hasn't performed any other year either. Just stay."

Alex shook her head. She didn't have to explain herself to anyone, didn't have to make herself any more vulnerable than she already was.

"Enjoy the concert." She walked off before Riley could stop her.

Back at the bar, Hunter was bursting out of his skin to clock out and head to the park, where he was meeting his girlfriend. Once he left and Alex had finished putting the supplies away and locking the money in her office, she realized Riley was right. There was *no one* here. Most years, there were at least a few people who didn't care about the concert and preferred to pass the night in conversation over a couple of drinks.

She cleaned. She wiped down the bar and all the tables. She refilled the napkin dispensers and condiment containers. She swept the floor. She washed the chalkboard and rewrote the specials. When she was done, only half an hour had passed. She scoffed at the clock, tempted to throw something at it but not invested enough to replace it.

There was no avoiding it, was there? With no customers to serve and no friends to talk to, there was nothing here to distract her.

Twisting her lips in disappointment at her lack of willpower, she grabbed her laptop from the office, slid into a corner booth, and pulled up the livestream of Bridget's concert. If she couldn't avoid it completely, at least she didn't have to be around the entire town while she watched.

Bridget gulped down half a bottle of water and wiped her face with a towel before setting down her guitar and settling onto the piano stool. The crowd, though smaller than the ones she normally played for, cheered only for them. This was what she lived for. Not the adoration, just…the energy, that feeling of being alive that she couldn't get anywhere else.

She shared a private smile with Max, who knew how much she fed off this, before she said into the microphone, "All right, everyone, we've got one more song for you."

The crowd expressed their disappointment—loudly—and she took the opportunity to sneak a nervous glance at Max. He nodded. He was with her.

"Before we do that, though," she continued, "we have so many people to thank. To the whole town and everyone here, thank you for putting on this festival. The city council, I appreciate the work you do, but you could stand to pay your teachers more. Let's not make this a yearly thing." She paused to allow a chuckle from the crowd. "Thanks to my mom and brothers and sister-in-law for welcoming me home after I'd stayed away so long. My agent, Pippa, for not having a heart attack when I told her I was doing a free concert. Owen for setting up the livestream."

She pointed to him, Jordan, and Lu. Keiko was wrapped against Jordan's chest, a set of noise-canceling headphones dwarfing her tiny head.

"And Jordan and Lu for your forgiveness." Bridget took a deep breath. "And to everyone who's made me feel like part of this town again. I'm so sorry for staying away. I promise I won't anymore."

The crowd clapped and hooted at that.

She smiled. "Can you tell I'm stalling?" Off their laughter, she said, "Yeah, you can." She licked her lips and took another sip of water. "Well, the thing is—I'm stalling because outside of me and Max, no one's ever heard this song. It's about someone very special to me. A lot of people here in this park probably know what I'm about to say, but bear with me, please."

Max touched her elbow in a small but powerful gesture of solidarity.

"Her name's Alex," Bridget said, unashamed of the shake in her voice, "and she's the only person I've ever truly loved. But I made a mistake a long time ago, and I'm still paying for it today. God, there's so much I could say right now, so much I could apologize for. But I want to say those things to you, Alex, when I know you're listening."

An 'aw' ran through the crowd.

"Instead," Bridget continued, "all I'm going to say is I'm sorry, and I love you. I love you enough to want to make a future with you. And if you think you could feel the same way—maybe not tonight, but sometime down the road—then meet me at midnight. You'll know where."

She turned away from the mic to let go of a shuddery breath. She'd been scanning the crowd all night, but Alex was absent. She tried not to let it hurt, but it did.

If there was one thing that could take away that pain, though, it was music.

"This song," she said, "is called 'Alexandra.'"

On the piano, she played the intro, soft and somber. Then Max joined in on the guitar.

And Bridget sang, pouring herself into the song and hoping Alex would hear everything she'd never been able to say.

The sounds of the festival had died down as Alex walked down the sidewalk. She could've driven, probably should've driven, but she wanted the time to think. Still, she'd made no decision yet, really, about whether she'd even go into the theater.

Shortly after the concert ended, after Bridget had sung that song about her, her phone had blown up with texts from Lu, Jordan, Owen, Jaya, and even Evelyn.

She'd switched it off. She appreciated her friends' willingness to help, but she didn't need anyone else in her ear when she talked to the only other person who belonged in this conversation.

When she reached the theater, she slipped through the door with the broken padlock. Only to explain things to Bridget. She deserved that, at least.

The house lights were up, and Bridget sat in the front row. She stood when Alex came in and walked down the aisle to meet her in the center.

"Hi," she said. "I wasn't sure you'd come."

"I wasn't sure I would, either," Alex admitted.

Bridget had changed out of the flashy outfit she'd worn at the concert and into sneakers, her comfort jeans, and a Pitt sweatshirt. Her hair, pulled into a loose bun, was still damp from the shower.

She was breathtakingly gorgeous.

She was breathtakingly *normal*.

"Wait," Alex said, her train of thought veering off track. "Why are the lights on? *How* are the lights on?"

"I had the power reconnected. Can't do renovations in the dark."

"Renovations?"

A subtle flush rose to Bridget's cheeks. She lifted her shoulders in a shrug. "Yeah. I bought the theater."

Alex chuckled. Of course she did.

"I think it's sad the high school kids don't have an auditorium to perform their fall play and spring musical in. I'm not sure I'll get it fixed up in time for this spring, but eventually, that's the goal. And, you know, I'm sure we'll find other uses for it."

"That's great, Bridge. The kids are going to love it." Something sprang up in her heart, something small and fragile and hopeful. Did this mean Bridget was staying? Or, at the very least, would be around more than once every half decade?

Even if it did mean that, what would that mean for *them*?

"I hope so." Bridget shoved her hands into the pocket of her sweatshirt. "The truth is, you taught me a lot about my responsibility to the community. I'm sorry I've been slacking on it, but better late than never, right?"

"I'm sorry I was so harsh with you before. I was angry. I shouldn't have been." Everyone dealt with shit in their own way. If Bridget had needed to stay away from this town, stay away from Alex, Alex couldn't blame her for taking care of herself.

"And you're...not angry now?"

"No. I've thought a lot about what happened. I can't fix it, and we've both apologized till we're blue, so there's nowhere to go but forward."

"Forward..." Bridget stopped, took a shaky breath to compose herself. Her voice was barely above a whisper when she asked, "How come your forward feels so different from mine?"

Alex's throat tightened. "You have a life, Bridget, a life in a big city far away with important things to do. I can't tie you here, and I wouldn't be happy there."

Bridget ran her hands over her face. Then she stared at Alex. "You don't get to make that decision for both of us."

Alex licked her lips, desperate for a drink of water. "I finally understand now why you left that day. You did it for me, and I'm doing this for you," she said. "In today's world, what you do is important. You make people happy. You're a role model for teenagers who are questioning their sexuality or trying to figure themselves out."

Shaking her head, Bridget wiped away the tears that were starting to fall.

"I'm serious, Bridge. You can't just walk away from that."

Bridget walked down the aisle to sit on the edge of the stage. Once she was settled, she looked up. "You're an idiot."

Alex laughed softly. Yeah, she was. She ran a hand over her eyes and walked toward the stage, where she leaned against it. She shouldn't ask, but she did anyway. "Okay. Why am I an idiot?"

Bridget's voice cracked when she said, "Because I'd give up that life for you."

"You shouldn't have to. I don't want you to." It was true. Finding your calling in life was rare, and Alex would never take that away from Bridget.

"I don't need you to tell me what to do with my life."

"I know. I know." Alex rubbed her chin. This wasn't going very smoothly.

Bridget swiped a hand through her golden locks. "I think... I think we keep talking in circles and never really get around to what we mean. So..." She stopped, sighed, all the while never looking away from Alex's gaze. "So, I'm going to say what I want and how I feel."

Alex's breath stopped in her throat. She'd never been more terrified in her life.

"I know what I want, Alex," said Bridget. "I don't have to think about it. Because what I want is *you*, a future with you, and I don't care what steps we have to take to make it happen or how hard those steps are." Voice gentle, she said, "I know you, Lex. I know you're afraid of getting hurt again. I wish I could promise I'd never break your heart, but no one can promise that. All I can promise is to try to love you as much as you deserve to be loved."

She took Alex's hand, intertwined their fingers, and looked up to make sure it was okay.

Alex didn't pull away.

"I love you," Bridget whispered.

Alex pushed the breath out of her lungs, inhaled, and repeated. She had known—somewhere deep down—it was coming, and still she wasn't prepared. Maybe she would never be prepared.

"The only question is," Bridget continued, "do you love me, too? Do you want to make this work as badly as I do?"

"That's two questions," Alex murmured, because she couldn't handle the burgeoning hope in her chest. The life she'd pined for, convinced herself she'd never get, was within her reach. Within *their* reach. So why couldn't she take that last leap?

Bridget hopped down off the stage and moved a step closer, bowed her head so their foreheads touched and her breath fluttered over Alex's cheek. "Let's... Let's stop punishing ourselves. Haven't we done enough of that?"

They really had. Alex tightened her grip on Bridget's fingers. "I don't need you anymore," she said softly. "I haven't for a long time." When she was seventeen, when she was twenty-three, she'd thought she couldn't live without Bridget. Now she could. She'd proven that.

Bridget's chest heaved. She looked down at their locked hands. "I know. I know that." She brushed a lock of hair behind Alex's ear. "But isn't that the making of a good partnership?"

Alex closed her eyes and inhaled deeply. Her voice came out small "I'm scared."

Bridget cupped her cheek, brushed her thumb back and forth. "I know, baby. So am I."

Alex pulled back, just enough to look into Bridget's eyes. "You are?"

"Of course I am," Bridget said, smiling tearfully. "There's nothing more terrifying than putting your heart on the line. But I want to be brave for you. I'm going to be brave for you."

Alex bit her lip. If they were both going into this with open eyes and pure intentions, that already increased their odds. Didn't it?

"Be brave for me," Bridget whispered. "Be brave *with* me."

Alex saw truth and courage and hope in Bridget's blue eyes. "I don't need you, but I still want you. I always will," she said, surprising even herself. "And I promise to wake up every morning and be brave enough to choose you, to choose us."

Bridget's eyes watered. There was a question there, one she couldn't quite give voice to.

And Alex couldn't quite give voice to the answer. She brushed her thumb along Bridget's cheek and leaned forward.

It really all came down to one thing.

Maybe they didn't need to fix who they were, to painstakingly pick up the pieces of their hearts and glue them back together in a clumsy approximation of what used to be. Maybe what they needed to do was take all those fragile pieces—the fragments of both their hearts—and create something new.

Bridget closed the distance between them. This kiss was different, neither desperate nor reverent. It was solid and stable, an inevitability, two pieces coming together, never to be parted again.

Alex's head spun. "Come home with me?" she murmured against Bridget's lips. "Not...not to have sex or to rush anything. I just want to be with you."

Bridget changed into the plaid pajama pants and oversized T-shirt that Alex gave her, brushed her teeth with a spare toothbrush, and slid into Alex's bed, sitting up against the headboard to wait for her. Benny, who'd been zooming between the two of them, left Alex in the bathroom and jumped up on the mattress. He lay down beside Bridget and licked her face.

"Hey, buddy," she said. "I've missed this, too."

Alex came out of the bathroom in basketball shorts and an oversized sweatshirt. She grinned at the sight of them cuddled up on the bed. "Benny," she said sternly but with affection, "it's my turn to cuddle her. Sorry, bud."

Whimpering, Benny stood up as Alex climbed into bed. Bridget scooted so she was near the middle, and Benny settled on her far side. They sat with shoulders touching, a quiet calm surrounding them. Bridget didn't know what to do next.

Alex set her hand, palm up, on Bridget's thigh. Bridget took it, entwined their fingers, and snuggled into Alex, who dropped a kiss on her head and ran her fingers through her hair. All the tension drained from Bridget's body. This was where she was meant to be.

After a few minutes, Alex asked, "So, how'd it feel?"

"The concert?"

Alex lifted one shoulder. "Doing something good for your hometown. It's thanks to shitty planning that we've let ourselves get into this mess, but you saved people from having their taxes raised, and you saved their kids from having to suffer from substandard education because we can't afford to pay teachers what they're worth. That's pretty noteworthy in my book."

Bridget shifted to look at Alex. "I didn't do it for them." After everything they'd gone through, she didn't know why this was so hard to say.

Alex squeezed her hip, the contact reassuring and grounding.

"I did it so you'd be proud of me," Bridget said.

Alex pressed soft kisses to Bridget's brow, her cheek, her ear, her lips. "Why don't we make a promise," she said, "to try our best to be gentle and to be good—to ourselves, to each other, and to everyone around us?"

With a smile, Bridget said, "I think I can handle that."

Judging by the weak sunlight outside, Alex woke a little after dawn. Solid arms encompassed her waist, blonde hair tickled her shoulder, and warm breaths puffed against her neck. Alex smiled. Her heart was full and sated, and she never wanted this moment to end. But it would, and that was okay because there would be many, many moments like this in the future. She was still scared, still terrified actually, but that fear wouldn't rule her life anymore. Instead, she would overwhelm it with love, warm and solid and grounding.

Bridget groaned when Alex slid out of bed, but Alex pressed a quick kiss to her temple and retreated into the bathroom. On her way back, she noticed both their phones on the nightstand lighting up with silent notifications. Tucking herself under the covers again, she picked up hers.

There were countless messages and social media notifications, the majority of them bearing a link to a clip of last night's concert. Smiling, she set the phone back down, curled into Bridget, and nuzzled her nose against her neck.

"Bridge," she murmured.

Bridget stirred without opening her eyes. "Hmm?"

"You're viral."

"What?" Bridget asked, voice thick with sleep.

"There's a clip on YouTube of your last song from yesterday. The speech before it, too."

Bridget groaned.

Alex let out a breathy chuckle. "You're not embarrassed, are you?"

Bridget opened one brilliantly blue eye. "'Course not. I just don't really want to share my vulnerable moments."

"Maybe you should've thought about that before you did it."

Humming and closing her eyes again, Bridget scooched closer. "That would've been hard because I was only thinking about you."

Alex warmed from the inside out. This happiness she felt now was akin to what she'd experienced at eighteen, at twenty-three. But it was more mature, more measured. It was for life.

She pressed a gentle kiss to Bridget's lips. "I love you," she whispered.

"And I love you," Bridget said, "but I'll love you more after a couple more hours of sleep."

Alex just laughed, kissed her again, this time on the cheek, and closed her eyes.

Chapter Fourteen

Now

BRIDGET AND ALEX ARRIVED FOR Sunday dinner together, hand in hand, bearing wine and flowers. Her mom greeted them with too-tight hugs and an admonishment that they didn't have to bring anything. Bridget waved her off and led Alex into the living room. It was a full house tonight—both her brothers, Jaya, the kids, Lu, Jordan, Owen, and little Keiko, who'd officially become a handful since mastering crawling. It was chaos, the exact kind of chaos Bridget loved.

"When are you two headed to New York again? I want to visit," Jordan asked over dinner.

Although New York was still her official home base and Alex visited occasionally, over the past three months, Bridget had been spending less and less time there in order to be with Alex as much as possible. She was also overseeing the theater renovations and making an effort to be more present in the town. This was the easy part, though, since she was in an ebb period of writing and recording the new album, which meant she wasn't on tour or in big demand for interviews or appearances. The respite wouldn't last too much longer.

"Not that soon," Alex said. She looked at Bridget. "We could probably be persuaded to do a long weekend, though, and show you guys around."

"For sure. I'd love to," Bridget said. She squeezed Alex's thigh. "And I've finally managed to get this one to agree to be my date to the Grammys, so we'll be in Los Angeles next month."

"How glamorous," her mom said.

Alex groaned. "That's what I'm afraid of."

There'd been growing pains, of course, from trying to merge their separate spheres, and the Grammys would be their biggest test yet. Bridget wasn't worried.

She pressed a kiss to Alex's cheek. "It'll be fun. We'll make a weekend of it, go sightseeing. The Grammys will be a minor blip in the adventure."

After dinner, the frigid January weather prevented them from going outside to play with Arya and Dev. Instead, they built a fire in the living room fireplace and taught them gin rummy while reruns of baking shows hummed in the background, volume turned low.

In the corner of the couch, Bridget snuggled against Alex. The room around them faded away as Alex leaned forward to kiss her softly. It was barely a kiss, but to Bridget, it spoke volumes. Warmth flooded her, and she smiled against Alex's lips. Even though she preferred to profess her love in song, she liked Alex's ways, too.

Bridget was practically vibrating with excitement as she waited on Alex's plane to land. The Grammys would be their first public outing, and she was equal parts ecstatic and nervous. Ecstatic because she'd get to see Alex after a week away and spend the next four days with her. Nervous because Alex was super private, and Bridget couldn't predict how she'd react to all the attention.

As much as Bridget loved her fans, she didn't always relish being recognized in public. But today, it proved to be a blessing, as taking pictures with preteen girls and being asked about her girlfriend by baby gays was the only thing taking her mind off the fact that Alex's plane had been delayed not once, but twice.

Her followers on social media were loving her saga of waiting in the airport. She'd taken selfies at the food court and in different shops and lounges captioned with things like: *My girlfriend's plane is delayed, and I'm wandering this airport until she gets here. Here's a picture of flight attendants knitting while they wait for their next plane.* Videos, too—of herself singing along to one of her songs playing over the loudspeaker or little interviews and interactions with folks who were also waiting for their loved ones.

It'd been fun, but also, *where* was Alex? She was going crazy here. God, how did she ever go five years without this woman when a week had driven her mad?

When the plane finally landed, it was another ten minutes before the passengers could depart. The whole time Bridget waited, she was bouncing on the balls of her feet, craning her head over the emerging passengers for a shock of curly brown hair.

Then she saw her.

It took every ounce of willpower not to run through the crowd. When Alex was clear of them, though, she opened her arms for a hug, and Bridget took the opportunity to leap at her, knocking her back a step.

"It's only been a week," Alex said, laughing into Bridget's neck and dropping her bag to lock her arms around Bridget's waist.

"It's been ages. I've missed you!"

"I missed you, too."

Alex kissed her deeply, uncaring about the people swirling around them. Bridget sank into the kiss. She'd always thought of home as a place, but the past four months of jetting all over the country had her realizing that no, *home* was just a synonym for *Alex*.

"I love you in suits," Bridget said.

Alex turned away from the mirror to face her. They were in a hotel suite in downtown LA that was so luxurious it had her head spinning. More than that, Bridget's sparkling green gown with its plunging neckline was *doing things* to her. She grasped Bridget's hips and purred, "Why do you think I chose it?"

Bridget let out a hearty laugh before kissing her soundly. Alex, feeling the heat build in her belly, groaned into the kiss.

"Oh, my God," Bridget said as she pulled away. "I know what's going on in your head, and we do not have time for that."

"I can't help it my plane was late," Alex whined.

Bridget's eyes sparkled with mischief. "I'll make it up to you tonight. Promise."

A few minutes later, when they were settled in the limo, Alex's phone dinged with a text from Lu. There was no message, just a link to a cellphone video of them making out at the airport that afternoon. Her cheeks went hot. "Oh, God," she muttered.

Bridget leaned over, took one look, and laughed. "I'm not going to lie. That probably won't be our last make-out to grace the home page of a gossip site."

When the limo arrived at the Staples Center, Alex sank back into the seat with a groan.

Bridget clasped her hand. "Nervous?"

Alex nodded.

"Don't be," Bridget said with a squeeze of her hand. "I got you." Then she led Alex out of the limo and into the crowd, where they were instantly overwhelmed by shouting and camera flashes.

And even though Alex's heart was beating a mile a minute and she was already sweating through her suit, she'd never felt safer.

"You made it!" Owen cried as he spotted Alex coming down the aisle.

Bridget, as part of the pit band for the high school's musical, had needed to be here pretty early, so Alex had sent her off with a good-luck kiss and gotten ready alone. The theater still needed some minor work, but it was a usable space for the kids, even if the paint was so fresh the fumes couldn't be totally masked.

Alex greeted Owen with a hug. "You got a babysitter!"

"It's a big night. Couldn't pass that up."

"Thanks for coming. I know Bridget really appreciates the support."

"Of course. We all came." He gestured to the row, which they'd managed to completely fill.

Jordan, Lu, Riley, Evelyn, Marcus, Ian, Jaya, Arya, Dev. They were all here. Alex waved to everyone in turn before scooting into the row and sliding into the seat they'd saved for her between Lu and Evelyn.

Evelyn gave her a side-hug. "Nice to see you, darling."

"And you."

The pit band was warming up and tuning their instruments. Bridget sat in the back at the keyboard. Like the rest of the pit, she wore black jeans and a black T-shirt. She'd even roped Max into this, although Alex suspected he liked small-town life just as much as she did and welcomed the change from the city.

Bridget looked up from her sheet music.

Alex held up a hand in a small wave.

When Bridget saw it, she broke out in a grin.

Alex settled back in her chair. She attended the production every year, both to support the high school and for something to do in this small town, but this was the first year since she'd graduated that she had more than an idle interest. And she was proud of Bridget—for doing right by the hometown that treated her so well, for giving the kids a role model to look up to.

The music began, and the curtain opened, and Alex sat back to enjoy the show.

A few weeks later, Alex was in the front row of the studio audience of an entirely different type of show, *The Mikayla Miles Show.*

"Bridget," Mikayla said as they settled into their chairs, "so nice to see you again."

"And it's nice to be here," Bridget said with a wide smile.

Alex was always slightly in awe of how winning Bridget was during television appearances. Of course Alex found her charming no matter what, even at six AM with messy hair and morning breath. But it was odd—a good kind of odd—to see her how the general public reacted to her.

"It's been, what, six months since you last visited?" Mikayla said.

"Yeah, that sounds about right."

"And so much has changed for you since then. You're no longer based in New York, you have a new album coming out at the end of the summer, and, most exciting of all, I think, you're in a relationship. I know that's what everyone's most curious about, but outside of a few appearances together, you've been pretty tight-lipped."

Bridget actually blushed. "Probably to your dissatisfaction, I'm going to remain tight-lipped about that except to say that we're happy. Deliriously so."

Heat rose to Alex's cheeks, too. Bridget sought her in the crowd and, when her gaze settled on Alex, sent her a dazzling smile.

Mikayla didn't miss the moment, but gracefully, she steered the conversation to a different topic. "You've been open about your bisexuality for a while now, but in a way, it's a lot more visible now. What do you think your visibility means to your fans in the LGBT+ community?"

"You know, I really hope it makes them realize that life *can* be good and you *can* find love, and that for so many people, differences don't have to divide us," Bridget said. "I want to write songs for people like me. I want teenage girls to be able to sing about the girls they have crushes on, whether it's in the privacy of their bedroom or in a bowling alley or wherever. I want boys who are coming to terms with being gay to recognize themselves in a song. I want non-binary kids to hear a song with they/them pronouns and realize it's normal. I just want to give them a little hope because I was in their situation once upon a time."

The audience clapped, and Alex, smiling, joined them. She didn't always appreciate the attention they got while in New York, which was one of the many reasons she preferred the quiet of their hometown, but the moments when they interacted with Bridget's young queer fans made it worth it. They clearly needed an example like she and Bridget could give, needed songs like the ones Bridget and Max wrote.

"Well, you're certainly an inspiration," Mikayla said when the clapping had subsided. To the camera in front of her, she continued, "We're going to take a break, but stay tuned! Bridget and her writing partner, Max Ocampo, will debut the first single off Bridget's upcoming album after our commercial break."

As Bridget moved to the stage where Max waited, she passed in front of Alex.

Alex mouthed, "Love you," and from the softness in Bridget's expression, Alex knew she understood.

"I'm exhausted," Bridget groaned. After a month of promoting the new album, she felt like she was sleepwalking. All she wanted was to sleep for a day. Maybe two whole days. And then there was the tour to focus on.

Alex unlocked the front door to her house. She'd come home three weeks ago to catch up on her businesses and had just picked Bridget up at the airport. Benny greeted them enthusiastically, his tail whipping wildly.

Alex helped Bridget out of her jacket and hung it on the hook in the foyer. "Why don't you go upstairs, and I'll bring you some tea?"

"Are you sure? You've got to be as tired as I am."

"Not quite. It'll take three minutes. I'll see you upstairs."

"Okay." Bridget kissed her on the lips. "Thank you."

Upstairs, she changed into pajamas and settled on her side of the bed, Benny jumping up after her. This was her life now, and the normalcy was all the sweeter for almost having lost it. There was only one thing missing. *She* was ready, but was Alex?

Did Alex even want it?

Bridget calmed herself by petting Benny, and a few minutes later, Alex came up the stairs with two mugs of steaming tea.

Alex stripped out of her jeans and sweater and donned her sweats. She was as gorgeous as ever, and love welled in Bridget's heart as she watched. Because she'd been blessed in a lot of ways, but this was the tops.

She didn't want it to be a big production because Alex wasn't like that. Alex was simple and caring, and she deserved something considerate. So there would be no bended knees or hot-air balloon rides or jumbotrons at baseball games.

Since Bridget had moved in, the end table on her side of the bed had been full of books. The drawer, though, contained only one thing, a ring box. She retrieved it now, while Alex was distracted by getting into bed, and held it under the blankets.

Beside her, Alex settled, grabbed her mug from her end table, and blew on her tea. "It's good to have you back."

"So good." Happiness seeped out of Bridget like warmth. Phone calls and text messages and Skype sessions could tide them over for a while, but Bridget craved nothing more than Alex's presence.

Bridget sipped her tea. It was comfortable. It was home.

"Are you happy?" Alex asked, her voice soft, almost hesitant.

Bridget lifted her head to meet Alex's gaze. Almost a year in, and they'd made it work just like they'd promised to. And they *talked*. That was the most important thing. They told each other when they were upset, when they were tired, when they were frustrated, and they always worked things out.

"Yeah, I am," she said. "Are you?"

Alex nodded. "Mm-hmm."

Bridget pressed her lips to Alex's, reveling in the familiar, reassuring touch. When the kiss ended, Alex rested her forehead against Bridget's.

Bridget could stay here forever—in this bed, in these arms. She took a deep breath. She was going to do it. She was. "Good. Because I have something to ask you," she said, pulling away.

"Okay..." Alex raised an eyebrow and sipped her tea. "Are you going to ask me to move in with you?"

Bridget rolled her eyes. "You're ridiculous."

"Ooh, no," Alex said. "You're going to ask me to bake my famous cake for your birthday, aren't you? Bridge, I was going to do that already."

"Are you going to stop guessing so I can ask?" Bridget said, lips curling upward.

"Fine. I'm sorry. Ask away," Alex said, setting down her mug.

Bridget's fingers locked around the velvet box. She pulled it out from under the blankets, opened it to show the modest ring, and set it in the space between them. She took a huge breath. She had so many words planned, so many sentiments to share, but Alex's brown eyes were full of love and nothing else seemed to matter too much in this moment.

Bridget took one of Alex's hands. "Alex," she said, "I love you. Through all the hectic days, I always have you to come home to, and I'm so unbelievably grateful for that. I want to spend the rest of my life with you, making memories and just *being* with you. Marry me?"

"Hold on a sec," Alex said, slipping out of bed.

"Are you kidding me?" What was happening right now? Bridget was asking the most important question of her life, and Alex wasn't even paying attention.

"I'll be right back!" Alex opened her sock drawer and fumbled through it.

Bridget rubbed her eyes. "I'm trying to propose to you."

"I know that." Alex, fist clenched, hopped back in bed.

"Are you done?"

"I'm done."

Bridget wanted to be mad, but there was an earnestness in Alex's gaze that made her anger and confusion dissipate in a heartbeat.

Alex uncurled her fingers to reveal a similar-looking box, which she opened to reveal a square-cut emerald ring.

Bridget gasped softly. "Your grandma's ring."

"My grandma's ring."

Bridget looked up, tears pooling as she registered what this meant. "That's a yes?"

"As long as yours is, too."

Their lips crashed together, although they were barely able to keep the kiss going because Alex was grinning and Bridget was cry-laughing.

"I love you, Bridget Callahan," Alex murmured as she slipped the ring onto Bridget's finger. "I love our life together."

Bridget did the same for her. "And I love you, Alex Marlow, and this life we've built."

Alex held her hand beside Bridget's, her thumb interlocked with Bridget's pinky so both of their rings were in view for Bridget to snap a picture.

"Who are you telling?" Alex asked.

"Just my mom and brothers and Jaya and Max," Bridget said.

"Can you make it a group message and add Lu, Jordan, and Owen? I think they'd like it if it came from you."

"Liar. You just want it done so you can have your way with me."

Humming, Alex bent her head to pepper kisses on Bridget's neck. "Do you object?"

"Absolutely not. But they'll kill us if we don't answer our phones until morning."

Alex grinned. "They can take it up with us at dinner tomorrow. We can take bets on who's angriest at us for not telling them in person."

"It's going to be Owen, easy," Bridget said. "What kind of bet is that?" She sent the picture, along with a dozen heart emojis as the caption, to the most important people in their lives.

Then she turned off her notifications. They had way more important things to do. Alex's arms were already around her waist, coaxing her backwards, and Bridget, smiling into the kiss, went willingly.

About Charley Clarke

Charley Clarke writes romance, both contemporary and speculative fiction. She loves baked goods, long walks, and relaxing with a good book and a cup of tea.

CONNECT WITH CHARLEY

Website: www.charleyclarkewriter.com
Twitter: @CharleyCWriter

Other Books from Ylva Publishing

www.ylva-publishing.com

Face It

Georgette Kaplan

ISBN: 978-3-95533-976-0
Length: 198 pages (70,000 words)

Ten years ago, Elizabeth Smile had one sizzling night with her roommate that left her craving more. Now her friend has reappeared with an odd request: Will Elizabeth play her fake girlfriend for a family Christmas in Ohio? The deal comes with a suspicious sister with her own agenda and the digging up of Elizabeth's old feelings. A twisty lesbian romance about getting more than we bargain for.

A twisty lesbian romance about getting more than we bargain for.

The Art of Us

KL Hughes

ISBN: 978-3-95533-890-9
Length: 218 pages (79,000 words)

When Charlee met a leggy brunette with a valedictorian medal hanging from her rear-view mirror and an attitude as biting as a Boston winter, it was love. For four years, she and Alexandra were unbreakable…until they weren't. A chance meeting years later sweeps them up in a whirlwind of heart-rending history. Is it too late? Or should the past remain the past?

Hearts and Flowers Border

L.T. Smith

ISBN: 978-3-95533-179-5
Length: 291 pages (71,000 words)

A visitor from her past jolts Laura Stewart into memories—some funny, some heart-wrenching. Thirteen years ago, Laura buried those memories so deeply she never believed they would resurface. Still, the pain of first love mars Laura's present life and might even destroy her chance of happiness with the beautiful, yet seemingly unobtainable Emma Jenkins. Can Laura let go of the past?

Hearts and Flowers Border is a simple tale of the uncertainty of youth and the first flush of love—love that may have a chance after all.

Hold My Hand

AC Oswald

ISBN: 978-3-95533-686-8
Length: 187 pages (66,000 words)

When Bethany and Savannah split up, Bethany is heartbroken. But a year later they meet again and their feelings are as strong as ever. So why did Savannah leave her?

Bethany is devastated by the answer and realises she will lose Savannah again—to cancer.

In a world where time is fleeting but love lasts forever, Savannah and Bethany can only hold each other and live their dreams.

Always a Love Song
© 2019 by Charley Clarke

ISBN: 978-3-96324-198-7

Also available as e-book.

Published by Ylva Publishing, legal entity of Ylva Verlag, e.Kfr.

Ylva Verlag, e.Kfr.
Owner: Astrid Ohletz
Am Kirschgarten 2
65830 Kriftel
Germany

www.ylva-publishing.com

First edition: 2019

Credits
Edited by Alissa McGowan
Cover Design and Print Layout by Streetlight Graphics